Answered Prayers

Answered Prayers

Tiffany Zweifel

RESOURCE *Publications* · Eugene, Oregon

ANSWERED PRAYERS

Resource Publications
An Imprint of Wipf and Stock Publishers
199 W. 8th Ave., Suite 3
Eugene, OR 97401

www.wipfandstock.com

PAPERBACK ISBN: 978-1-6667-3148-4
HARDCOVER ISBN: 978-1-6667-2403-5
EBOOK ISBN: 978-1-6667-2404-2

10/28/21

To my friends and family who always believed in me and encouraged me. And to my Father in Heaven who makes all things possible and answers everyone's prayers.

Contents

A Day at the Beach

WINSTON JAYMESON GROVER CRESTED the towering wave hurtling toward shore. Bikini-clad teenagers, middle-aged women in Hawaiian-print cover-ups, even fellow surfers, all craned their necks around striped beach umbrellas to get a better view of his ride. As the wave curled and broke, Winston crouched, bent his legs, grabbed the sides of the surfboard, and dove onto his stomach, riding the foam to the beach. He jumped off when he landed, then hauled the heavy board to the cabana he shared with his friends.

"Hi, Winston! Taking a break from studying today?" Laura, a red-haired beauty asked from her reclined beach chair.

Winston had been coasting through law school for years. Really, he didn't see the point. He was just trying to keep his dad happy and postponing the inevitable. It was easier to be a student—even a law student—than an actual lawyer. Both his father and grandfather before him had worked around the clock. Billing. Billing. Billing. Sure, they stockpiled assets—boats, wineries, condos, beachfront homes, estates, country club memberships. But for what? Rarely did his father and grandfather enjoy them. His mother and grandmother weren't happy either. They had their society friends and got to show off, spending whatever money they wanted, but what they really wanted was to feel loved. And the only way to feel loved was to have a spouse spend time with them. The message they got was that they weren't nearly as important as money—or even the client. They were just trophy wives. Look good. Stay on the shelf. Don't do anything important.

Winston was uncannily attuned to everyone's moods. He felt the restlessness, the discontent, the disillusionment. He didn't want any part of that lifestyle.

The pendulum had swung.

On the opposite spectrum from his predecessors who saw their relationships through golden anniversaries and beyond, Winston had bounced from one girl to another and one irresponsible thing to another. And even though he didn't consider himself obsessed with money, he still had plenty of it. Why not enjoy? He grinned and nodded at Laura.

"Want to play some more beach volleyball?" his friend Dave asked everyone in the cabana, twirling the volleyball over and over, obviously itching to play.

"Maybe in a few," Winston answered. He flopped onto a padded lounger and reached in the cooler for a drink.

"I'll play," Jennifer told Dave, and more friends got up to join them, following like a pack of geese.

Winston took a long drink and scanned the horizon. Lots of children. Lots of families. Lots of hot girls. Which one might be fun to ask out this weekend? His gaze settled on a couple close to where the waves lapped the shore. The woman was slim, pretty, and wore a conservative black-and-gray one-piece. She was trying to wade into the water, but the man kept grabbing her roughly by the wrist.

With her downcast eyes and hunched-over demeanor, the woman showed every sign of being abused. Winston felt his back stiffen and couldn't peel his eyes away. The man threw her down on a blanket. His finger stabbed the air, pointing to a picnic basket, and she immediately began setting out their lunch.

Uncomfortable, Winston looked away, watching his friends laugh as Laura went for the volleyball and badly botched the shot. The ball bounced off the head of a sunbather, who sat up and rubbed the spot, looking around grumpily.

"Sorry!" Laura called, scooping up the ball. "Are you okay?"

The man stared at the vivacious redhead in the tiny bikini and quit rubbing his head. "Oh, sure. No problem. Didn't bother me at all," he said, practically drooling as she walked away. Instead of lying back down on his stomach, he sat up and watched the rest of the volleyball game.

Winston smiled, then looked back at the couple. The man's mouth moved furiously, but not chewing, as Winston would have expected. Instead, he was yelling at the woman, who seemed even more withdrawn, like she hoped the sand would swallow her. She looked up, pleading for something. *Oh,* Winston realized. *She wants to go out in the water.* She kept looking at it longingly. *Help her.* The thought came urgently, but he pushed it away. *Maybe after I eat,* he thought.

He started to reach into the bucket for another piece of chicken, but he had the strongest urge to help the woman first. Sighing, he pushed the bucket away, then strode over to the volleyball game, grabbing Dave and an extra ball. He explained the situation to Dave, suggesting a bit of a distraction. As they approached the couple, the woman had finally made it to the water and was wading up to her knees. But the man still gripped her wrist.

"That's far enough!" the man barked at her.

"But, Gary! We've come all this way. Can't I just take one small swim?" she pleaded meekly.

"No! Let's go. I knew coming here was a mistake, just like everything about you is a mistake, you no-good idiot!"

Whoa! Winston knew this guy was a jerk, but he was downright cruel. And in that instant, Winston knew this situation was way worse than a controlling boyfriend denying his girl some enjoyment. This was an extremely abusive situation. In his gut, he knew he needed to do something. He felt a swell of seriousness come over him. The playfulness he'd felt with Dave disappeared, replaced with steely resolve.

"Did you hear that?" Winston asked, his mouth a grim line. "You need to hit him way harder than we planned. This is no mere distraction to allow that girl to swim. I think this might be a rescue mission." The truth of it rocked him to his toes.

Dave froze, mouth momentarily agape. His demeanor also changed as he quickly assessed the situation. The woman had small bruises all over her body. One eye looked smudged and a bit swollen. The wrist the man had grabbed looked darkened with bruises.

Dave nodded. "Are you seeing what I'm seeing?"

They had to help this woman.

Dave immediately started selling the act by trying to explain to Winston that spiking the ball was easy. "You just use this motion, like this. Then you throw the ball," he said. When they got in range, Dave spiked the ball right at the jerk, who dropped like a rock. "Bull's-eye!" Dave muttered and turned to give Winston a triumphant grin, but his friend was no longer there. Dave bent down to the man, blocking the view of the ocean with his body. The man sat up, dazed, then scrambled to crane his neck, searching for his girlfriend, but Dave kept getting in his way.

In his best beach-bum voice, Dave said, "Sorry, dude! That ball got away from me. I didn't mean to even hit it. And I especially didn't mean to hit anyone. Are you ok, dude?"

When the man fought even harder to find his girlfriend, Dave grabbed his arm and started hauling him to the first-aid tent.

The man loudly and roughly protested. "Let go of me, you idiot! I need to find my wife! She could get swept away by these large waves."

⤷ ⤶

Alexandria had been looking forward to the Los Angeles trip for months, her heart rippling with both fear and anticipation. She knew Gary would feel obligated to his parents to come, and since they both needed fertility testing, she couldn't be left in South Dakota. He wouldn't have left her alone anyway. She also knew a crowded beach or sidewalk was her best chance for escape.

For a year and a half, morning and night, she'd prayed she would be able to escape. "Dear God in heaven, please help me to get away." Her heart would flutter with fear, so she also prayed for strength.

It all happened so fast. She had begged Gary to let her take a few steps into the ocean. She was enthralled by the constantly moving, crashing, churning waves. The immense expanse of ocean fading into the horizon was the liquid version of the flat open South Dakota prairie. She asked Gary if he would go with her, but he refused, saying the surf was too rough and dangerous. She promised she would stop as soon as it hit her knees. She heard a bit of commotion behind her. It sounded like Gary was yelling at her. Maybe if he was afraid of the water, she should run out farther, use this to make her escape. But where would she go? How far could she get? Gary would be waiting for her when she got back to shore, and then she would really be in for it.

Trust me, came the soft, piercing voice she had become familiar with for the past year and a half.

Then someone was right beside her, and a man's voice gently whispered in her ear. "Do you need help escaping from that man?"

Before she could answer, he was gently but quickly escorting her back to shore. What was happening? Her first impulse was to pull away, to push this stranger away, to yell that she didn't need his help and explain how Gary was her husband. But while her brain tried to tell her tongue what to say and her legs what to do, she heard the soft voice repeat, *Trust me. Go. I am answering your prayer.*

She glanced at the man beside her. His lips were not moving. She felt a warmth spread through her that had nothing to do with the blazing sun overhead.

A calmness swept over her. And she knew.

Her prayers had been answered.

Chapter 2 ——————————————————————————

An Answered Prayer

"Yes, help," she whispered, her mouth finally catching up with the sudden shift in her reality.

Her pace quickened to match his. He carried a large robe with a hood. In a flash, he had the robe around her, covering her hair.

"Ok, now, let's slow down," Winston said softly. "Hold my hand. I think we are far enough away and I got you covered up before he could see which way you went. My friend Dave caused a distraction. Now we are going to head right to my car."

Alexandria fought the urge to look back. Like Lot's wife in the Bible, she too could be destroyed with one last look back. But the temptation tugged at her. His expression would be one of bewilderment and anger. Oh, how she would love to see that prideful, arrogant beast injured and knocked to the ground in a beautiful reversal of roles and fate.

But she resisted the temptation. She clung to the fact that her prayer had been answered. God had looked out for her. Now she refused to do anything to jeopardize her newfound freedom. Almost in a stupor, she marveled at what was happening.

From the day she had become trapped in a loveless marriage of servitude and abuse, literally a prisoner in an isolated home with no car or telephone, she had looked forward to this like a distant dream. She'd never thought it would come true. Her mind could scarcely comprehend it, but her heart soared with hope.

⌒ ⌒

Winston felt a thrill when they reached the car. *We did it!* he thought. But just as quickly, a new thought invaded his mind. Now what? Was he going to just take her to his house? Take her to the police or a women's shelter?

He pulled away from the parking lot, the euphoria quickly ebbing into stark reality. Why was he always so impulsive? Why did he so often interfere in other people's lives? Why did he get himself into these messes, and how would he get out of this one?

The woman was shaking, even in the thick terry-cloth robe. First things first, he thought.

"What's your name?" he said gently.

Staring at her hands, she said, "Alexandria."

"Alexandria," he repeated. "That's a beautiful name."

She shook her head.

"You don't think it's a beautiful name?"

She shook her head again.

"My name is Winston. Don't you think that's a ridiculous name? Winston Jaymeson Grover. Most of my friends call me Winston. Most of my enemies call me Winnie or Winnie the Pooh."

⌒ ⌒

Alexandria laughed nervously, finally looking at her rescuer for the first time. She noticed that he had bleached-blonde hair, a bit wavy and mussed, golden tanned skin, a warm smile to match, and soft brown eyes. He was looking at her with concern. No man had ever looked at her with concern like that. Warmth replaced the chill, and her shivering stopped. She couldn't recall ever seeing such a handsome or friendly face.

"If you don't like the name Alexandria, how about shortening it to Alex, or Andrea, or Allie? Or we could come up with something else."

"Allie . . . I like that," she answered. "Alexandria sounds far too pretentious. I only liked it when my mother said it. But she died a long time ago."

"Who was that awful man you were with? I saw him grab your wrist and yell at you."

Allie took a deep breath. "My husband, Gary. A monster. I've been praying for over a year that I could escape. And you . . ." She timidly glanced up at him. "You were the answer to my prayer."

Winston was more rocked by the news that the man was her husband than that he had been an answer to her prayer. A husband further complicated matters. Winston was a third-year law student. Although it was increasingly easy to get a divorce these days, this monster husband could make things messy.

"Do you think you could get a divorce?"

Allie looked at him without guile or pretense or an agenda. She shook her head. "No. He would never grant me a divorce. He would never settle for half the ranch when he could have the whole thing. I think he likes having someone to control and to hurt, to cook and to clean for him. He's going to search for me. But not because he loves me. Because he *owns* me. And I think, just by leaving even for a short while, when he finds me, he will kill me. But I'd rather be dead than ever live with him again. I think that's why he didn't want me to go into the water. He was probably afraid I would try to drown myself."

Winston gulped. The man was totally psychotic! What had he just gotten himself into? Could he get out as easily? But then he looked at Alexandria—no, Allie—and felt a wave of sympathy, followed by a steely resolve to see this through. He had to see it through. That awful beast of a husband had absolutely no right to treat his wife that way, and Winston was going to stop him.

He looked at the frail, bruised, and beaten—but not broken—woman beside him. "Do you seriously think he would kill you? Maybe we should go to the police."

She turned her soft hazel eyes on him, looking at him directly for the first time. "That would never work. You don't know him. He is smart and conniving. Somehow, he convinced even my own mother to believe him instead of me. I have no chance, none, of having the police take my word over his. I don't know how he does it."

"Your own mother chose to believe him over you? How did that happen?"

Allie shook her head, her eyes downcast once again. "He fed her lies. And she believed him. He told my mother I was the one lying." Allie covered her face with her hands and started to cry.

Winston pulled over, put the car in park, and reached over to lay a hand on her arm to comfort her. He was startled when she flinched and pulled back. "Oh, your bruises!" he exclaimed. "I'm so sorry. Did that hurt you?"

❦ ❦

She could only stare at him. Her mind tried to process this new way of interacting, of being. This man was trying to help her. He was trying to touch her in a way not meant to hurt but to comfort and console. Her mother hadn't even comforted her since Gary had turned her against her daughter. No one had. Well, sometimes in the beginning, Gary had shown a little tenderness, but at even the slightest hint of rebellion or unwillingness or independence from Alexandria, Gary had squashed her. Now, he just pummeled her over and over and over.

Allie shivered.

❦ ❦

Still alarmed, Winston started driving again. He made up his mind. He could not leave such a timid, abused woman to any legal institution or shelter. The system could at times be broken and untrustworthy. While it did a lot of good, too often, people like Allie fell through the cracks. He could not take that chance. He could only rely on himself and his friends. Perhaps even his family. So he was taking her home.

"Allie," he said with steely resolve. "Am I correct that you never want to go back to your husband?"

"Never," she said softly, then louder. "Never!"

As Winston mulled over that aspect of her situation, the puzzle pieces seemed to fall into place. He pulled over again and picked up his phone. "I'm going to call Dave. With the help of my friends, I think we can make you disappear forever. Would you like me to try?"

She nodded, and he speed-dialed Dave. "Hi. The situation is even worse than I thought." Winston quickly filled him in, glancing at Allie, who sometimes looked down at her hands and sometimes at him with hope-filled eyes.

"Can you have someone report that they tried to rescue a woman they thought might be drowning?" He glanced at Allie again, reminding himself what her swimsuit looked like. "She was wearing a black-and-gray one-piece and has brown hair. Having the specifics of her description should help prove the caller is reporting the correct person. In any case, we need to help her disappear for good."

Chapter 3 ——————————————————————————————————

Searching

DAVE DIDN'T ASK ANY more questions. He had seen firsthand the abuse inflicted by the creepy husband, and now he had further evidence. He'd agreed to the plan Winston suggested, shared it with his group of friends, and chosen the friend least familiar with Winston to make the call.

Police and lifeguards now swarmed the beach and water as the search continued, blue-and-red emergency lights illuminating the area in the fading light. Onlookers, with their umbrellas and picnic baskets stowed away, couldn't tear themselves away from the unfolding drama. Gary Tackleman marched angrily between the policemen and rescuers, demanding they find his wife. Dave wondered if he was aware of the ugly welt that had formed on the back of his head. He was probably feeling the headache that accompanied it, though.

Aaron, the lucky friend who had been elected to call 911, stood in the midst of the chaos. Again, he pointed in the direction he had spotted a woman facedown in the water.

"And why didn't you call or alert authorities right away?" the policeman asked. Gary Tackleman, the woman's husband, was glued to his side, frantic. His eyes pierced Aaron, who shivered under the unspoken accusation, like it was Aaron's fault the woman had disappeared and the man would soon be getting his revenge.

"I honestly didn't know if she was swimming or drowning. She wasn't thrashing, you know?" He looked at the officer with questioning eyes. The cop nodded. "I watched for a long time to make sure she surfaced. When she didn't, I tried hard to find her. I looked all over. She had just vanished! I didn't know what to do. I talked to the lifeguards. They wanted me to call you while they looked for her. So I did."

"But my wife disappeared an hour ago! I called the police before you did!" Gary shouted with such force that every officer and lifeguard nearby looked stunned. "What took you so long?"

Aaron gulped. "I told you. I was searching for her. I figured she was swimming or snorkeling, and I was trying to determine if she was okay before I raised the alarm. Then I was searching for her."

An officer put out a calming hand. "That is what lifeguards are also trained to do. You did just fine. It is unfortunate Mrs. Tackleman is missing. We will keep searching until we find her."

"If she drowned, shouldn't she have washed up on the beach by now?" Gary yelled, causing everyone to cringe. This was his wife he was talking about.

"Are you saying your wife was not a good swimmer?" the officer inquired politely.

"She was a decent swimmer, I guess. But I felt like the surf was rough today. Some of the waves were huge. She could have got sucked out and then drowned. I tried to stop her from going out at all, then some knucklehead smacked me with a volleyball and knocked me down."

Aaron started to grin but quickly smothered it.

Gary continued. "I tried to find Alexandria right away, but the idiot tried to haul me to the first-aid tent, and I had to shake him off before I could look for her. I haven't seen her since. But I can't believe with all the people here that she hasn't been found." He glowered at everyone.

The police officer looked solemn. "Sir, we hope to find her. Alive, of course, but if that isn't possible, we hope to find her to bring closure to her family. We will do our best. We know of many cases where beachgoers have been swept out to sea and then rescued by boaters. Don't lose hope just yet."

Among the searchers scattered along the beach, only Aaron knew her body would never be found.

Chapter 4 ————————————————————————

A New Home

As if waking from a dream, Allie climbed out of the car, shut the door, and truly looked at it. What a nice car. Then she looked at the house and did a double take. The solid gray stone was interspersed with tall, stately windows. Lots of windows! Well-manicured shrubs forming perfect triangles lined the walkway. A fountain with sparkling water adorned the center of a circular driveway. The sophisticated wrought-iron and glass doors were set behind a solid porch. Allie gaped. She felt a bit like Cinderella arriving at the ball. At the stroke of midnight, the beauty and serenity would disappear and, poof, she would be scrubbing floors in misery as Gary's upraised hand threatened to put her in her place.

That gave her an idea. "Is this your house?" she asked meekly. "Could I clean your house—be your housekeeper?"

Winston considered. She *could* work as a maid. In Southern California, you could sometimes dodge questions about maids and documentation. They were usually paid in cash. Allie could hide from her husband indefinitely. But that would mean she would just be shut away in another house. She would be trading one prison for another, he thought.

No, he wanted her to truly experience life. He could set her up in a home of her own, maybe help her find a job—something she enjoyed doing. Or maybe she could go to college and share an apartment with Jenna, Katie, and Sailor. He and Jenna had dated seriously but then realized they weren't meant to be. They remained close friends. He could trust them. But was that best for Allie? Maybe she should remain here for a while. Could he somehow help her to transition? He wasn't sure what to do.

Allie looked at him expectantly. Finally, he said, "We'll see." Allie looked disappointed. Maybe she was afraid he was rejecting her. "Let me show you the house." He reached out to comfort, guide, and welcome her, but she reflexively backed away from his outstretched hand. Winston lowered it to his side. He couldn't blame her. On the drive, when talking had ceased, he had discreetly studied her. She was covered in bruises. Fortunately, she had naturally darker skin, but it was discolored in a shocking array of purple, gray, green, and even yellow, depending on the age of the bruise. Winston tried to imagine what her life was like. Not even her own mother believed her. She was completely alone, without a friend in the world.

Well, she had a friend now.

"Come on. I will show you around," he repeated.

She followed behind him, mouth open, head swiveling to take it all in.

He bounded up the winding circular staircase with Allie gripping tightly to the polished banister. They peeked through each door at empty bedrooms, an office, and an exercise room. He had her briefly look inside his enormous master bedroom with its masculine four-poster bed and massive armoire, dresser, and wardrobe.

Winston was still showing Allie the upstairs rooms and deciding which one to have Allie move into when the doorbell rang. Allie stopped, expecting Winston to run down and answer it, but he continued the tour.

"Shouldn't you go answer the door?" she asked.

"Huh?" Winston opened a door and was entering a palatial guest bathroom of glass, chrome, and glitter. It was bigger than her kitchen.

"The door?" Allie repeated. "I heard the doorbell."

Winston waved a hand dismissively. "Sebastian will get it."

"Who's Sebastian? Your dog?"

Winston whirled around and burst out laughing. Well, Sebastian did sound like a dog's name, he thought. "Sebastian is my butler. He answers the door."

Winston heard the shrill, nasal voice and froze. He looked at Allie nervously. "Could you stay here a minute? Make yourself at home. This will be your room and bathroom."

༄ ༄

"I'm going to stay here?" she asked incredulously. "Oh, good! You decided I can be your maid after all, with room and board." She felt her heart lift with hope. "What a wonderful room, Winston!"

She felt the heavy burden of fear dissipate, replaced by the heady exhilaration of freedom and the opportunity to work for this nice man. She felt a physical change when she thought she might never have to see Gary again. It took every bit of self-control and biting the inside of her cheek to keep from yelling and bouncing up and down and throwing her arms around her rescuer.

∽ ∾

Winston shook his head. That wasn't what he had in mind. True, she needed help, but he wanted her to be able to find her strengths, explore her talents, gain experience, and discover hidden abilities. He didn't want to hold her back from reaching her potential—whatever that might be. She was not going to be his maid, he decided. But she wasn't paying attention to him.

A sudden commotion halted them and had them looking at each other in confusion. The bedroom door was forcefully slammed against the wall. They came out of the bathroom in time to see a tall, lanky, glamorous woman burst through it. "Winston!" she yelled in a high-pitched voice. "What are you doing, and who's this?" She gestured distastefully to Allie.

Sebastian stood stiffly and uncomfortably behind her in the hallway and anticlimactically announced, "Miss Elizabeth is here."

Elizabeth stood there staring at Allie, who was still dressed only in her swimsuit and the oversized robe. Winston had hoped to avoid this confrontation until after he had figured out what was best for Allie and had answers for Elizabeth. Now he felt like he had done something wrong. The trio stared awkwardly at one another.

Sebastian stepped in and cleared his throat. "Miss Elizabeth, meet Miss ..."

"Allie," Winston supplied.

"Miss Allie, this is Miss Elizabeth Thorpley, Winston's girlfriend."

Bless the man, Winston thought.

Allie gawked at this woman. She must have come straight from a photo shoot with *Vogue*. She had smoky eyes with dark, spiky lashes, her long hair was smooth and sleek, and her lips glistened with red lipstick. Wide hoop earrings added a touch of glamour. And that was just her face.

Allie's eyes traveled to her long, leggy, perfect figure. The clothes were well cut and made of a material that was so light it seemed to float.

∽ ∾

Winston watched as the two women took each other in. He noticed how Elizabeth scrutinized Allie's stringy mop of still-damp hair. That frumpy robe made her look like a kid's playdough project. But her features were obscurely fine and regular, enhanced by lots of shadowing. Or were those bruises?

Allie stood watching in awe. Elizabeth was disconcerted.

"Who are you?" Elizabeth demanded again, striding up to Allie and practically poking her in the nose with an artistically manicured nail.

"I'm the new maid," Allie said softly.

Winston was suddenly glad he hadn't gotten around to clarifying that misconception with Allie.

"The new maid, huh?" She whirled on Winston. "I didn't know you were in the habit of giving your maids a tour of the house. And while wearing a bathing suit. Did the tour start at the swimming pool?" A beautifully shaped eyebrow quirked up, the full lips pouting.

"This is a special case," Winston stated honestly.

But as soon as Elizabeth had heard "maid," she no longer cared about the rest of the story. It was all too tiresome. Allie had ceased to be a threat. In fact, she ceased to be noticed at all.

"Winston, I came to see if you wanted to go out to dinner tonight." She looked him up and down. "My word, you look a mess! Go get cleaned up so we can go." She flapped her arms at him, trying to shoo him into the shower.

Winston glanced at Allie, who seemed mildly entertained, like she had stepped into a soap opera. In a way, she had. "Since when do you eat dinner?" he asked.

"I eat," she whined annoyingly. Winston had been itching to break up with this stuck-up snob but had enjoyed the celebrity of being seen with the popular model and hated to give that up. He glanced at Allie. Time to put Elizabeth to the test.

"Elizabeth, I need to be honest with you. Allie is not here to be my maid. She is here as my guest. So I am happy to go to dinner, but she is coming too."

"A guest? What do you mean? Why did she say she was going to be your maid?"

"Because she thought that was what I intended, but, well, it's a long story," Winston answered.

∽ ∾

Alarmed, Elizabeth again studied Allie and again quickly decided she was no threat. A long story? How tiresome. Elizabeth didn't want to be bothered. Winston looked a mess, plus he was insisting this woman tag along on their date? No way! If she couldn't have a quiet, romantic dinner with Winston looking good enough to attract attention and make other women jealous, it was not worth the trouble.

"Never mind. I didn't think you'd be looking like such a wreck or have company. I'll just grab some Thai takeout on my way home." She was already leaving, turning away on her impressive silver stilettos. "Call me tomorrow," she called over her shoulder as she brushed through the door. It was a command, not a request.

∽ ∾

Winston stared after her, surprised and relieved. Sebastian still stood there. "Yes, Sebastian?" he asked. Sebastian had a good reason for everything he did.

"Sir, would you like me to send Sarah to buy some clothing for your guest, or something more immediate from your own closet, maybe?"

Winston looked at Allie again. Of course, she wouldn't have anything but the clothes on her back, and it was only a scrap of clothing at that. He pulled out his wallet, thumbed through its contents, and extracted five $100 bills. Handing them to Sebastian, he said, "Thank you! Could you find her some pajamas and clothes for tomorrow? I will take her shopping for more then."

"Of course, sir." Then he leaned in and whispered something. Winston felt his cheeks warm and nodded. Sebastian cleared his throat and hurried off, holding the stack of bills. Allie was too embarrassed to ask. Maybe Sebastian remembered she would need underwear. She hoped so!

The awkward moment was interrupted by Winston's cell phone. He answered it as he left the room, heading down the hallway and downstairs.

"Winston, it's Tessa! My friends and I were just wondering if you wanted to go clubbing in L.A. tonight? Blake was afraid you had plans with Elizabeth, but we thought it was worth a try."

Winston was torn. Unlike dinner with Elizabeth, this was tempting. Tessa, Blake, and Cynthia were lively and gorgeous, and they were amazing dancers. Their charm, good looks, and connections got them into all the hottest clubs. Among the many offers and invites Winston received in a weekend, one from this trio was prized. Oh, how he wanted to say yes. He looked up toward Allie's door. He couldn't just leave her alone on her first night away from her husband and what he hoped would be her old life.

"Tessa, Tessa, Tessa, you know it kills me to have to say no," he started to explain.

"Then don't!" she exclaimed.

Winston groaned. This was so hard to turn down. He thought of many wild weekends he'd danced with all three hotties at once, every guy in the place looking at him with jealousy, admiration, and even respect. Laughing uproariously, the four would dance the night away. He would even have a few other gorgeous women slip him their phone numbers as they coyly smiled and disappeared from the room. The music was always incredible. The vibes couldn't be beat. Besides, what was he going to do here? Have milk and cookies with a married woman who was scared of her own shadow?

He was just about to accept when the door to Allie's room opened and she poked her head out, looking up and down the hallway, then down the grand spiral staircase to the foyer, where she spotted Winston. Their eyes locked. Hers looked lost and bewildered. She must be questioning her rash actions of the day, he thought; actions that he, Winston Jaymeson Grover, had instigated and which had led to this dramatic turnaround in her life.

"Winston? You there? You coming tonight?" Tessa's voice sounded far away as the moment of eye contact between Allie and Winston stretched out.

Winston had made his decision. He snapped back to the present. "Tessa, I have had something really important come up. Maybe I can tell you about it sometime. But meanwhile, you girls have a wonderful time on the town tonight."

Like slices of Domino's pizza around teenage boys, the playfulness vanished. Tessa understood and didn't argue. Her serious tone now matched Winston's. "Anything wrong? We can scratch our plans and help you instead. What is it?"

Winston was touched. Most people thought Tessa, Cynthia, and Blake a shallow bunch. Maybe her offer wasn't sincere, but at the moment, it sure felt like it. What Winston really needed to do was assess the situation. What could he do to help Allie start a happy new life? As soon as he knew, he could start asking trusted friends and family members for help and advice.

First he needed to find out who was trustworthy. What if he told the wrong person and they went to the police and her husband found out? She'd been serious when she confided that if he found her, he would kill her. And Winston had seen the anger on his face as he'd grabbed her wrist, fully intending to inflict pain and suffering. Oh yes, he had been very successful in inflicting pain on Allie.

"Thanks, Tessa. Your offer means a lot. It's serious, but I am not sure how you could help. If I get that figured out, can I count on you?"

"You sure can. Are you positive I can't do anything right away?"

"Positive. You girls go have a great time tonight."

"Ok, Winston. We'll miss you. Best of luck with everything. Truly." She disconnected.

Allie descended the stairs. She looked distressed. "Winston, did I ruin your plans again?" She stared down at her hands.

Winston laughed. "Ruin, no? Change, yes," he said honestly. "We need to talk, get some things figured out." He looked around the spectacular foyer. They needed some comfort food and a cozy, quiet place to talk.

They made sandwiches with gourmet bread, meats, and cheeses, and added a few munchies. He led her into the family room, where they balanced plates on their laps while being swallowed by the enormous leather couch. Allie looked like she was melting into a giant cube of butter.

"So," Winston said after most of their meal had disappeared. "Tell me more about yourself."

Chapter 5 ────────────────────────────

Allie's Story

ALLIE COULDN'T REMEMBER THE last time she'd felt so comfortable. The last time someone had taken care of her was probably when she was fifteen. Her mother had brought her some soup and made her take the day off after she'd rolled her ankle from a fall off a horse.

She stared at her hands and then looked up at Winston. Although he was a large, muscular man, she didn't feel the least bit afraid. Instead, she felt warm and alive, secure and protected. This would take some getting used to, she thought. The tension she always carried in her shoulders now relaxed. Her shallow breathing had gradually deepened throughout the day. The instinct to flee vanished.

"I don't know where to start," she finally confessed.

"Just start at the beginning. Where were you born? Do you have siblings? Did you go to school?" he coaxed.

"I was born in Sioux Falls, South Dakota. I'm twenty-two, by the way. I grew up in Mitchell, well, in the country near Mitchell. I went to school there."

"Near Mitchell? So you were isolated? How far were your nearest neighbors?"

"Yes, very isolated. Growing up, the nearest neighbor was less than two miles away, but now I think the nearest neighbors actually live in Mitchell, which is about eight and a half miles away."

"Eight and a half miles. Wow! That is isolated. Sorry, go on."

"So, we lived on this ranch. My father, mother, and me. I had a brother who was killed in a freak accident. We had this terrible windstorm and my father sent him out to wire the gate more securely. A cottonwood tree fell, a large branch hitting him. It was awful. I was seven years old, and my brother was twelve when it happened. My father was never the same after that. Before the accident, he used to laugh a lot. He would pick me up and swing me around. Trips into town included ice cream and visits to friends and neighbors. After the accident, he was grouchy and sullen. If I asked for help with my homework, he would yell that he was too busy and ask why I was so stupid I couldn't do my homework. I quit asking for help and didn't do well in school because he was right. I *am* stupid."

Winston held up his hands in protest. "Allie. I don't want to hear you refer to yourself like that. You are not. And I'm going to prove it. I feel like your father probably didn't recover from the traumatic experience of losing his son. He probably blamed himself because he was the one who sent him out into the storm. In fact, I bet he told himself he was stupid over and over. He couldn't get past it and took it out on you. It's so sad."

"Maybe," she said quietly, looking distant and thoughtful. "Anyway, by the time I was twelve, my father was working sixteen-hour days to keep the ranch running, and it took its toll on him. Our nearest neighbors were the Tacklemans." She paused to see if that registered with Winston, but then she remembered she hadn't told him her last name. "Joe Tackleman ran the neighboring ranch with his son, Gary. They started helping more and more. After I finished eighth grade, my father insisted I drop out of school to help on the ranch. He was becoming more and more sickly and frail."

Winston didn't move, didn't speak.

"So I spent all my time feeding and watering the cattle, moving them from pasture to pasture, and mending fences."

"How big was your ranch?" Winston asked.

"Only about 1,200 acres."

Winston whistled. "That's a large spread. How many head?"

"Also about 1,200. Of course, it increased every spring by about five hundred, and I had to be on hand to make sure the calves were delivered without a problem."

"And if they didn't?"

"I would usually have to get Gary or Joe Tackleman to help me. But they couldn't always get away from birthing their own cows. So then it got . . . messy," she said, shrugging.

"Wow!" Winston said, looking at this petite and bruised woman in fascination. "So, basically, you were what? A thirteen- or fourteen-year-old girl running a 1,200-acre ranch with very little help?"

"My mother had to step up and help. I never did it alone. But if I hadn't quit school, we would have been forced to sell, and my father was too stubborn to do that. Our land had been in the family for four generations. But my mother was also trying to care for my father, who was steadily going downhill, as well as care for the home and fix meals."

"Did your father get better? What did he have?"

"I don't know. But it was pneumonia that finally took him a few years later. On his deathbed, he insisted I marry Gary Tackleman."

"He's the creep from the beach!" Winston exclaimed.

Allie nodded.

"How were you forced to marry that jerk?"

"Well, my father never left the house. Besides my mother and me, he only saw the Tacklemans. They were good to him. Good to us. They helped us all the time. But Joe and his wife, Betty, were in their seventies and ready to retire somewhere warm like Florida or Arizona. They wanted to sell their land to pay for retirement. Gary wanted to buy the land from them, keep the ranch going, but the bank wouldn't back his loan."

"But he was their son," Winston said. "Couldn't they just let him keep the ranch and pay them off as he was able? One day he would inherit the money anyway, right?"

Allie shrugged. "I don't know the arrangements. But I do know this: Joe and Betty were almost fifty years old when Gary was adopted to help run the ranch. I think they felt like Gary owed them something because they'd adopted him, instead of the other way around."

Winston frowned. "That's not right, getting free labor and using Gary like that." *This is a tragic story on all counts,* he thought, *and about to get worse.* He set his empty plate on the end table and turned his attention back to Allie.

Allie shrugged again. "So then everything happened at once. The Tacklemans sold the ranch and moved here to California. Gary moved into our bunkhouse and became our ranch hand. Then my father got pneumonia, and his dying wish was that I marry Gary so his ranch would be taken care of."

"His ranch? Didn't he want you to marry Gary so his daughter was taken care of?"

"No. His ranch," she confirmed. "My mother was also highly in favor. Gary treated her with the utmost kindness and respect, like what they called brown-nosing at school. Even I was starting to warm up to the idea, even though I was only seventeen and Gary was almost twenty-six. So I married him." She sighed. "The abuse started small—so small my mom dismissed it entirely. Then, as it became more pronounced, I had welts and bruises. Gary would tell my mother I was lying about where they came from, and he would make up a story like I was rammed by a bull, or I fell off my horse, or the fence post had snapped and hit me in the face and that was why I had a black eye. My mother never saw his dark side, so she didn't believe it existed. Plus, she knew I did not love Gary. I didn't even like Gary, and so she thought I was making it up as a way to get rid of him."

"You never even liked Gary?" Winston was incredulous. "So is your mother still alive? Is she back on the ranch?"

Allie looked stricken. "Oh, Winston, it was so awful," she said in a quiet voice. "About a year and a half ago, she collapsed. Gary and I had been out working the cattle all day and didn't find her until late. We loaded her in the car and took her to the hospital. They said she had cancer throughout her body, and they were surprised she had managed to hide it from us for so long. She must have been in severe pain all the time."

"That is awful. Did they do treatments?"

"No, it was too late. Gary insisted we bring her home so we didn't have to pay additional hospital costs. She lasted four days. The day she collapsed and was left unattended and dehydrated took a severe toll."

"Allie, I'm so sorry for your loss. And was Gary even worse after she passed?"

"Oh, yes. Horrible. Always abusive. It was horrible. Before, I used to go into town with my mother on Saturdays to shop for groceries and other things, even go to lunch. On Sundays, we would go to church, maybe a picnic. Gary would run into town whenever he felt like it, and I enjoyed the break. But when my mother died, Gary hid the keys. I was no longer allowed to use the car. He also disconnected the phone—not that I had anyone to call. He became paranoid. He started spreading rumors among some of his friends that he was worried about me. He meant for the rumors to circulate around town."

"What kind of rumors?"

"Rumors meant to keep me from escaping the horrible marriage. I hadn't kept in touch with friends and had dropped out of school after eighth grade anyway, but I did have one friend. I told her Gary was abusive and I wanted to divorce him and get away, but she laughed and said Gary was right. I asked right about what, and she said he'd warned everyone I would spread lies about him being abusive. So I had no one to turn to. I was completely alone and at Gary's mercy. He got worse and worse and worse. This last year, I prayed and prayed that I could get away from him for good."

"And why were you able to come to California?"

"Gary's parents want to have a grandchild before they die. I have not been able to get pregnant even though we have been married for five years. Joe and Betty paid for us to fly to L.A. to do some fertility testing and then to visit them in Temecula. I'm pretty sure Gary thinks if he can provide a grandchild and appease them, he will inherit a large chunk of money and be able to buy the original ranch back. Then he will have three thousand acres, and with an outfit that size, he will be able to hire men to do the hard work."

"And did you already do the testing?"

"No, our flight arrived this afternoon, and the tests were first thing tomorrow morning. I made a bargain with Gary. I told him if he would let me spend at least two hours at the beach and see the ocean, I would fully cooperate with the tests and the remaining visit with his parents. He was fearful I would bolt and run to the authorities or tell his parents or even some strangers, but his parents forced him—us—into this trip."

"And would you have bolted or told somebody? I'm surprised he trusted you enough to make the bargain."

"I would have bolted the first chance I got." She looked Winston square in the eye and smiled. "And that is just what I did. But . . . like I said, I had been praying for a long time. For over a year. I had one Friend, and I talked to Him every day. Oh, Winston! It was the most amazing thing. I would be hurting and feel so alone, but then I would pour my heart out in prayer and feel this warmth spread from my heart and throughout my body. It was so warm and comforting. It was like a hug from God. And I would have these thoughts and impressions come into my mind." She was so wrapped up in her experiences she'd forgotten to be timid.

"Like what kind of thoughts?"

"Thoughts like 'I see all. I am aware of you. Be patient in your afflictions, and I will deliver you and take care of you. All will be well.' And, then, as the time got closer for our trip to California, I had these thoughts like,

'Pretend to be more submissive and accepting to build trust with Gary. If you do, escape will be much easier.'"

Winston looked dumbfounded. He remembered how he had heard, "Help her" and the strong urge to do just that. Could it have been God? Part of him believed, and part of him discounted the thought completely. It was ridiculous. Or was it?

He cleared his throat. "Allie, we need to discuss your future. Let's make your hopes and dreams come true. What have you always wanted to do?"

Allie looked puzzled. "For a job or for fun? What do you mean?"

Winston had been thinking job but was intrigued. "Both."

Allie leaned forward, her face brightening with excitement. "Oh, Winston, there are so many things I've always wanted to do! I still want to swim in the ocean. I want to ride on a boat. I want to go to Disneyland! I want to go to Paris and climb the Eiffel Tower. I want to go to London and see Big Ben and the House of Parliament. I want to ride a roller coaster. I want to go skydiving. Lots of adventurous things like that. But mostly, I just want a normal life. I want to have friends. Do you know I've never even been on a date? I never got to go to a school dance. In fact, I want to go back to school, maybe even go to college someday. And maybe, most of all, I want to fall in love and have a family."

She looked up at Winston in wonder, excitement, and joy, and he couldn't ever remember seeing a face more vibrant or beautiful, not even among his bevy of model girlfriends. The eye contact sparked with energy, and Winston couldn't tear his eyes away.

Finally, Allie motioned to the TV. "Do you think they would have anything on there about my disappearance?"

Winston snagged the remote and flipped through several channels, then looked at his watch. "I think we missed it. But let me call Dave." He pulled his phone out.

"Dave. What's the latest?"

"I just heard from Aaron. He took some heat for not reporting it sooner. He did his best to convince them that the woman he saw was drowning but that he was still uncertain enough to cover his bases and keep himself out of trouble."

"It hadn't occurred to me that having him tell the authorities that he potentially saw a drowning victim would come back to bite him—like shooting the messenger. But Aaron was able to give them the details about her hair color and swimsuit?"

"Oh yeah, Aaron said the jerk husband practically jumped out of his swim trunks at the mention of those details. And I had to stay out of sight. Aaron said the jerk was ranting and raving about my little stunt with the volleyball and how it was all my fault his wife disappeared."

"Well, he's right." Winston chuckled.

"And how is the woman? Is she ok? Was her situation as dire as we thought?"

"Absolutely. We saved her from the worst of situations. But she is strong. She is going to be all right." He winked at Allie, but she was listening intently and looking at her hands again.

"I'm happy to hear it. Oh, and good news! Quick thinking by Aaron. He thought to get Gary Tackleman's contact information so he can follow up with him about the investigation. He said he felt responsible and wanted to check in on Gary to see how he was doing. But, really, he can help us keep tabs on the situation."

"Genius. Tell him I am grateful." He clicked off as Sebastian swept into the room, swaying under an armful of bags.

"Sebastian," Winston greeted, gesturing to Allie. "Much appreciated. Please take the rest of the evening off."

Smooth, cool-as-a-cucumber, unruffled Sebastian struggled to hide his surprise. "Thank you, sir. I hope everything fits, madam," he said, carefully setting the array of bags at her feet.

"No worries, Sebastian," Winston soothed. He knew Sebastian was a genius when it came to everything—including a woman's clothing size. "I'm taking her shopping tomorrow. But thank you for your quick thinking and taking care of our guest so promptly."

"A pleasure." Sebastian made a little bow and a wink that made Allie laugh. She opened the first bag and pulled out a pair of jeans and a soft sweater.

"I love it, Sebastian!" she said as he beat a hasty retreat. Winston knew he was quick to get clear out of earshot in case the boss were to change his mind.

Allie reached for the second bag. It said Victoria's Secret. She peeked inside, noticing what was probably three pairs of undies and a couple of bras. She hoped one would fit. Another bag had a pair of loafers and some socks. She reached in another bag that had some silky, satiny material and pulled out a soft, hot-pink pajama set. In the bottom of the bag were some matching slippers. She thought of the coarse, unstylish sweats and T-shirts she wore to bed at the ranch. She touched the soft material to her face. She couldn't believe how luxurious it felt against her skin. Suddenly, her swimsuit felt tight and chafing.

"May I?" she asked, gesturing to the clothes and looking around for the time. Should she change into pajamas or clothes? It was 8:45 p.m.

"Of course. Feel free to shower. Remember, that bedroom and bathroom up there are yours for as long as you are here. Sebastian, of course, will already have stocked it with towels, shampoo, a hairbrush, toothbrush, and toothpaste." He glanced down at his swim trunks, T-shirt, and flip-flops. Elizabeth hadn't been kidding. He did look like a mess! "I'm going to shower and change too. Then I will probably come back down and make popcorn and watch a movie. You've had quite the day, so you can either join me or go straight to bed. Your choice."

The choice is mine, she thought with a little shiver. She hadn't been able to make a choice of her own for a long, long time.

Winston smiled when she came down in her hot pink pajamas, hair a bit damp, and melted back into the couch, eagerly reaching for the bowl of popcorn. "What are we watching?" she asked shyly, and Winston's grin grew wider.

Chapter 6 ——————————————————

Appearances

ALLIE WENT TO GET into Winston's sports car to go shopping the next morning, but Winston shook his head, pointing to another garage stall.

"We're going to need that one," he said, pointing at the gleaming black SUV.

"Oh, is that how you shop?" Allie teased, and Winston burst out laughing.

She was so happy that it just spilled out. Allie couldn't believe she'd said such a thing to a practical stranger, but, oh, how refreshed and alive she felt, waking up in a cloudlike bed of fluffy white linens in her soft pajamas and with no demands to make breakfast or mount a horse to start fixing fence or feeding cattle. Today was Friday, the day she was supposed to go to the fertility clinic for all those tests. It was a delicious, heady feeling to play hooky like this. But she did worry about Mr. and Mrs. Tackleman. Would they worry about her? Would they mourn her? She wasn't sure. They definitely would mourn the possible loss of grandchildren. What would Gary do? Move on, marry someone else so he could still give his adoptive parents grandchildren and hopefully secure his inheritance? She shuddered for the poor woman who would take her place.

The SUV filled up as they shopped. Allie laughed lightheartedly for the first time in years. This was so fun. Winston was so kind.

They had such a fun day. Her stomach hurt from laughing so much, something she hadn't done in years. She felt herself shedding her shyness as easily as she had shed her old swimsuit last night. She felt a bit like a butterfly emerging from a cocoon. Part of her was afraid to expose this fragile new self, and yet she felt completely safe with Winston. Allie looked at Winston wistfully. What would it be like to live like this every day?

∽∾

After Allie went to bed, Winston clicked on the TV. He had set his DVR to record the news on all the major networks. He started with NBC. The red-headed reporter held the microphone tightly as she looked into the camera.

"Tonight, we are still looking for a missing woman, Alexandria Tackleman, who disappeared from a crowded public beach near L.A. yesterday. We ask for the public's assistance in this matter. If anyone has any information regarding the disappearance of Alexandria, please call the number on the screen. She was last seen wearing a black-and-gray swimsuit. Reports that she may have drowned have not been verified."

ABC seemed to be running the same segment they ran yesterday, with footage at the beach showing Gary Tackleman and search-and-rescue workers combing the beach as well as wave runners crisscrossing the water.

He rewound the news segment and froze it on Gary's image. The man looked upset but didn't have that glowering, mean look one would associate with someone so horrifically abusive. Perhaps he was the Ted Bundy type—charming, kind, good actor—someone no one would expect to be anything less than the concerned model husband. Winston wanted to puke.

Next, he watched CBS. They were interviewing Aaron. Winston sat up straighter and notched up the volume.

"I just wasn't sure," Aaron said uncertainly. "In the past, I've helped people who were thrashing in the water who I thought for sure were drowning, and they got angry with me. Plus, she was pretty far away. I thought maybe she was peacefully floating on her stomach. I sometimes do that. I looked away when a friend started talking to me. When I turned back, she was gone. But it kept bothering me, so I looked for her for a while, but she could have gotten out of the water while I was distracted. I just didn't know. Then I decided to report it—just in case. Surely, others were closer to her that would have helped her if she was actually drowning, though." He sounded doubtful.

Perfect, Winston thought. An eyewitness but with a hint of uncertainty. He definitely got the description accurate enough that people would see the match to the missing woman yet with enough ambiguity and distance that he couldn't be blamed for not doing anything or reporting it sooner—just a concerned citizen having a fun day at the beach but aware enough that someone might be in trouble and willing to do something about it.

He wished he could call Aaron, but he didn't dare. He needed to keep plenty of distance from Dave's friend just in case someone was watching. And Dave would let him know if anything changed. Winston sighed. The sooner people lost interest in the story, the better.

Chances were good the mystery would remain unsolved. If somebody had seen him leave with Allie, they probably would have reported it as soon as the story broke. The volleyball diversion had probably drawn the attention of nearby eyewitnesses. Plus Winston had quickly hidden Allie with the robe.

What about Elizabeth? he worried. Would all of her friends be abuzz about the news, and would Elizabeth key in on the fact that Winston's houseguest was, in fact, the missing woman? Probably not. Elizabeth would only watch the news if she thought she was going to be on it, he decided. If she did figure it out, though, would she call Winston first or report it to the police? He thought about it and decided she would probably call Winston first, demanding more information, wanting to know all the juicy details so she could brag or be spotlighted on the news. Sometimes her vanity was a good thing.

For now, it was best he keep up appearances that life continued as normal. And Winston had played hooky too many days in a row. He had an exam and a slew of tiresome appointments coming up, and invitations were piling up. Tomorrow, he would have to jump back in with both feet. But he would do his best to bring Allie along for the ride.

Chapter 7 ───────────────────────────────

Stir-Crazy

As the days passed, Allie grew stir-crazy. She wasn't used to just sitting around.

She felt useless. She didn't even have to do her own laundry here. Or her own cooking. Or shopping. Or anything, for that matter. Her every need was catered to, and she was bored. She wished Winston had made her the maid. At least she would have a purpose and something to fill her time. But she hated to bother him.

She did love spending time with him and found him fascinating. He was so unlike Gary. He had a hint of a dimple in his right cheek and wavy hair she wanted to reach out and touch. Winston's mouth quirked up at the corners, and his eyes danced with liveliness, as if life had been designed for his personal merriment. She could hardly look away from that face. And when she did, she found herself wanting to gaze at him again. He had an arresting charisma. Sure, he was handsome, but it was not the handsomeness that kept her gaze focused on him. It was more the happiness she felt when she looked at him, like he was letting her in on the secret joke. She felt drawn in. She liked being a coconspirator. There was an air of playfulness about him that made her want to giggle like a schoolgirl, and yet, when he listened to her, his demeanor turned serious, like every word she said was of the utmost importance.

∽ ∾

Winston thought Allie was beautiful. He was used to women bristling with confidence and self-importance—women who preened and groomed and flaunted their beauty. Allie was different. She was unaware of her beauty. She was shy, unsure, and quiet, but in a very appealing way. Her hair, which had been limp and shaggy the day they met and had probably never seen a professional cut, now glowed with a healthy shine and style. The eyes that had been so dull and lifeless now had a depth and warmth that came from overcoming hard things and the compassion of wanting to help others through hard things. Her bony, angular body had filled out to a shapely slimness. And her complexion had smoothed and lightened as the bruises faded and she wasn't spending every waking moment in the saddle. She had an innocent sweetness that made him happy to help her and protect her. He wanted to be a better man just by being near her. It was a heady experience.

When he first met Allie, she seemed to droop with dejection, stooped over like a woman triple her age, and she always looked down, both literally and metaphorically. But an amazing transformation had taken place. Her eyes glowed, her head was raised, her shoulders were back, and even her nose had a charming uptilt. Her mouth had flipped from a frown to a ready smile.

He could understand and sympathize with her boredom. He himself was used to being on the go. He had college classes and dental, chiropractic, and massage appointments. He had lunches with friends he always invited her to. He worked out at the gym and played golf with friends, students, or business contacts. He studied for the upcoming bar exam. And he went on dates with that horribly beautiful model girlfriend.

Although he couldn't yet take the chance of the wrong eyes spotting Allie, Winston invited her whenever he could. She had started going to the gym with him, and she enjoyed the workouts. He took her to the golf course and set up golf lessons for her while he played. She seemed to enjoy the lessons too. But she felt restless and useless.

She finally broached the subject one day when Winston was actually home for lunch.

"Winston? Could you please help me with something?"

"Oh, my. What have you prayed for now?" Winston asked, teasing her.

Allie's eyes sparkled. Her prayers *did* continue to be answered. She giggled, then sobered. "Winston, you've been wonderful to me. You rescued me. You've shared this beautiful home with me and bought me an amazing wardrobe. But I feel so useless. I don't do anything to help."

"You don't need to help," Winston said.

"I know. But I'm used to doing something. Working hard all day. Falling into bed exhausted at night. And while I'm grateful I'm not forced to work so hard, I'm feeling restless and without purpose."

"Oh? We need to find you something to do," he said matter-of-factly. He had been watching or recording all the news channels and hadn't seen a story about Allie's disappearance in over a week. "I can arrange that. Any requests?"

It was that easy? Just ask, and Winston would step in to help? She didn't know what to say, so she shrugged.

A cure for boredom, huh? Winston could always find something to do. "Want to do something today?"

Allie nodded again.

"Hold on while I make a phone call."

Two hours later, Allie's heart pounded as she looked out the airplane window. Flying to L.A. from South Dakota, she had enjoyed seeing the tiny houses and cars and people far below her. The little ribbons of shiny blue were large rivers. Trains that looked like toy sets circling Christmas trees actually carried huge loads of freight. Now, Allie looked at it from a new perspective. They were going to open that airplane door and walk into the empty nothingness and fall and fall and fall until they met those tiny, distant figures below. Of course, they would have parachutes to slow their descent. Winston had told her she would find the experience magical. She had told him she'd wanted to do this someday. But now that her chance had come, her heart pounded like a teenager's loudspeakers. What if the parachute didn't open? What if she didn't like the sensation of falling? What had she gotten herself into? Why had she told Winston she wanted to do this? She sighed. There was no turning back now!

"Ready?" Winston shouted above the roaring current of air buffeting the plane.

Allie could only nod. Her throat felt entirely closed off. At least she was strapped to a professional. Truly, all she had to do was endure this. Nothing to it, right? At least Winston looked eager and excited.

The skydiving instructor told her it was time. Another guy opened the door to the plane. Her eyes widened when Winston calmly went to the door and jumped out. Then it was her turn. Her instructor helped her to the door.

"On three!" he shouted. "One, two, three!"

The plane fell away, but above them. Allie's stomach dropped at about triple the rate as the rest of her body. Or maybe she had left it behind. She couldn't breathe as she looked at the ground below—a patchwork of green-and-brown squares and circles. She could see houses, buildings, warehouses, and pools of water. Still, they were falling and falling. Shouldn't they have pulled their parachute cord by now?

And then they did. And although they were still falling, Allie felt like they had suddenly shot up into the air instead. Then the rushing air around them stilled into an empty quiet.

There! She could see Winston's bright red-yellow-and-blue parachute a little below and to the right. Under its canopy, she could see he was waving at her. She waved back and gave him the thumbs up. The worst was over. She had survived the fall, and the parachute had opened. As she saw the world spreading below her, she felt peace and a thrill. Two weeks ago, trapped, bruised, broken, and bewildered in her tumbledown house in South Dakota, she could never have pictured herself here, in this moment, floating under an orange-and-green canopy among puffy cumulus clouds with a glimpse of blue ocean to the west. Her bruises had healed, her heart was on its way to mending, and her faded blue jeans and cast-off men's button-down shirts had been traded for designer jeans and silk. An abusive, rough, uneducated, and uncouth man had been replaced with one who was kind, intelligent, and refined. Allie decided then and there that if she were ever free of Gary, she would not and could not ever marry another man unless he was like Winston. She would rather be alone forever than settle for anything less.

Suddenly, her heart soared with joy.

Winston had literally opened the world up to her.

A Sand Dollar

"I HAVE ANOTHER SURPRISE for you today," Winston told her the next morning.

"Oh yeah? And what could possibly surprise me after skydiving?"

"Hey, yesterday you said you were bored," he joked.

"Skydiving wasn't quite the remedy for boredom I expected," she said. "Cleaning out your closet, pantry, or medicine cabinet is more my style."

Winston burst out laughing. "See? That is exactly why you need to stick with me. Instead of cleaning and taking care of future Angus steaks, I want you to say, 'Bungy jumping is more my style!'"

"Are we going bungy jumping?"

"No, not today, but that is a good idea. Maybe tomorrow."

Allie laughed until she realized Winston was serious.

"So what are we doing today? Did you say it was a surprise?"

"I think you will like it. Go change into your swimsuit and grab a towel and a change of clothes. Then meet me at the SUV."

"Ok." Allie couldn't wait to see what Winston had in store for her. She had been feeling cheated out of her one and only chance to experience the ocean. Was Winston aware of this? She had a feeling he did. He seemed to be aware and in tune with all of her needs. Her eyebrows knit together. She had been thinking so much about herself, but what about Winston and his needs? She had probably turned this man's life completely upside down, and she had hardly given it a thought.

"Winston? What would you normally be doing?" she asked.

"When? What do you mean?"

"Well, it's a Wednesday. Aren't you missing class or study time or job interviews? I don't know. Haven't I completely destroyed your schedule? Most people don't just have time to go skydiving or to hang out with some girl they rescued, do they?" She looked apologetic.

It was a legitimate question, and it floored him because he didn't have a legitimate answer. While he had good intentions of getting back to studying and launching his career in law, it had been far too easy to return to his old habits of wasting time and goofing off. How did you tell a woman who'd had to drop out of school at age fourteen to run a ranch, working twelve- to sixteen-hour days, six or seven days a week, that you pretty much didn't do anything? A conundrum, for sure.

"Allie, I'm still trying to figure that out," he told her honestly. "But today, what I'm doing is taking a special young woman out to experience some of the fun in life. How does that sound?"

࿂ ࿂

The sun fell behind them as they headed west, the traffic thickening with each passing mile. Two surfboards were mounted on top of the SUV. A picnic and a couple of floppy hats were stowed in the back, along with towels and a change of clothing for later. They arrived at the beach and parked, finding it fairly busy for a Wednesday morning. Winston climbed on top of the SUV, untying, then tossing down the two surfboards. Allie opened the back and pulled out the picnic basket and bags of towels and clothing. She threw them over her shoulder.

Winston watched with admiration. Without a word, Allie had efficiently packed up the gear. Elizabeth would have simpered and whined and waited in the SUV while Winston hauled everything himself. Maybe every guy needed to find himself a rancher gal, he thought with a smile and another admiring glance at his companion.

Initially, he had wanted to invite a bunch of his friends to make the day even more fun. But then he'd realized Allie would not have come if he had. He noticed she usually turned down invitations that involved a crowd—or even just one additional person. Was it shyness or distrust? Insecurity? The possibility that her secret would get out and Gary would find her? She certainly was not used to being around people. He hoped she would eventually learn to love being with friends.

Winston spread out a blanket, set up the beach umbrella, and arranged the gear with Allie's help. But she didn't want to sit on the blanket. She was itching to get wet.

"Can we get in, Winston?" she asked, shuffling impatiently, her eyes aimed at the sea.

She looked slim, vibrant, and radiant. What had happened to the girl covered in bruises who, only two weeks ago, was afraid to raise her head? Winston wondered.

Winston was stunned to realize that it was because of him these changes had come to this remarkable woman. Without his help, she would still be trapped with Gary, bruised, battered, and used yet neglected. Now she was happy and carefree, truly living life for the first time. He felt a sense of protectiveness, belonging, and satisfaction he had never felt before. He relished the feeling.

Now, to teach his little protégé how to surf. He followed a few steps behind her, smiling as she determinately strode into the surf and a rapidly approaching wave only to be knocked back as it broke over her. She squealed as the cold spray drenched most of her suit.

Behind her, Winston laughed in delight. She was like a small child enchanted by her discoveries. As the surf sucked the water back out, Allie quickly bent down and retrieved a sand dollar. She was so enthralled, flipping it over in her hand, that she almost got knocked over by the next wave. Winston was quickly there to steady her.

"What did you find? A shell?" he asked.

"Even better! Look!" She held out the round, fragile object for his inspection.

"Oh, a sand dollar." Winston smiled warmly at her.

"A sand dollar. What a great name. I love it."

Winston smiled. "Let me go put it in a safe place for you." Before he headed back to where their belongings lay on the beach, he said, "Now, Allie. You've got yourself in the danger zone here, where all these big waves are crashing on you. You should probably either stand back and let them splash your ankles or let the next wave take you a little farther out."

"Will I still be able to touch the ground if I do?"

"Mostly. But ocean water also makes it easier to float."

And with that, she was on the move, letting the wave carry her out like a delivery boy with Domino's. She was bobbing, floating, and jumping over each rolling wave. "This is so fun!" she squealed.

Winston couldn't help but laugh. He wanted to plunge into the water after her, but he knew Allie would want him to find a safe place for her fragile souvenir. He mused that she was a little like the sand dollar. Fragile, she had been buffeted by storms and waves yet had finally come to rest in a safe place where Winston was able to find her and tuck her out of harm's reach.

His mission accomplished, he felt a little giddy as he sloshed through the sand in his haste to join Allie. Her grin was wide as she bobbed up and down on the incoming waves.

"Look! I push off the bottom, then tuck my feet under me, and I ride on top of the wave. It's so fun, Winston!"

Winston stood beside her, mimicking her movements. It *was* fun, he thought. Allie had a way of making everything around him feel more fun. All the things he had taken for granted were new and exciting to Allie. That humbled and frightened him because he knew he wasn't living up to his privileges.

He pushed that thought away and grabbed a surfboard, ready to give Allie her first lesson. He described the process of paddling out, waiting for the big wave, and then catching it. "Let's have you practice standing on the board," he said. "I will hold it steady so you can get the feel of it."

Winston was pleased with her natural agility and balance. It probably came from riding horses. Together they tried and tried to help her catch her first wave, but they mistimed it, or the wave broke prematurely, or Allie's foot slipped. But she didn't give up.

What Winston saw in Allie's face was steely determination. She wanted it, and she wasn't going to let up until she got it. She gave it her all each and every time. Winston couldn't help but admire her. Why couldn't he get laser-focused like that? How did she do it?

After hours of struggle, they were both wrinkled like a couple of raisins and Allie was exhausted. But, oh, how he wanted her to experience what he did. Cresting a wave on a surfboard was like being on top of the world. He wanted to share that feeling with her. And suddenly he knew how he could do it—just like skydiving.

Allie crouched on the front of the board while Winston paddled like a madman. *Here it is*, he thought. "Hold steady," he shouted, and Allie obeyed. So did the wave. It broke at the perfect moment, with Winston poised at the lip, already standing, guiding, and balancing.

"Now!" he yelled, and Allie stood, feet splayed apart and hands outstretched for balance.

Allie just experienced the ultimate Titanic moment, and she did feel like she was flying—the wind in her face, the ocean spray on her feet, and Winston's hands gently encircling her waist.

She enjoyed it a little too much, and her lack of focus was their undoing. She tilted, Winston overcorrected, the board flipped, and this time Allie really was flying. She shot up in the air as Winston fell hard on the board. He splashed into the water, the wave broke, and Allie had a gentle landing in the cascading wave. Winston came up spluttering. Allie came down ecstatic.

"Winston! That was amazing! Today was the coolest day of my entire life! But now I'm starving. Is there food? Can we go eat?"

Winston laughed as he charged after his wayward surfboard. "You bet. I'm starving too." He rubbed the leg that had crashed down into the board. It might bruise, but boy, was it worth it!

While feasting on cold roasted chicken legs, green grapes, French bread softened and warmed by the sun, crackers, cheese, and sodas, the two recounted the amazing moment they were in sync enough to ride a surfboard in tandem.

"The ocean's even more amazing than I thought it would be. And I had really high expectations," Allie said.

"It's always been one of my favorite places," Winston admitted.

"Did you bring my sand dollar up here?" she asked.

He pulled it out, and she examined it. Earlier, Winston had thought about how Allie was so much like that sand dollar—fragile, beautiful, and in need of protection. But after what he experienced with her today, he altered his thinking.

A sand dollar was just an empty shell. Allie was very much alive. He couldn't keep her as a souvenir. He needed to let her go. She needed the chance to live her own life without a domineering man pushing her into what he saw fit just to fulfill his own needs. And she wasn't as fragile as he thought.

Over and over throughout the day, he replayed her asking, "What would you normally be doing? Do you usually attend classes? Study? Go to job interviews?"

Winston had needed this lift, this reminder. His father had always made him feel worthless, like he wasn't capable of doing anything worthwhile or taking care of himself, and so he sent his best employees to care for his son. Winston had been dragging his feet. When the message came in loud and clear that you weren't worth much or you couldn't run the company as well as your father did, one couldn't help but believe that message.

But Allie was sending him a different message—that he *could* make a difference. He *did* make a difference.

No more dithering. He was going to pass the bar. He was going to start handling cases, even if he started at the bottom, even if he worked for someone besides his father so that he could do his part and make a difference. He was going to break up with Elizabeth. She only wanted him for appearances anyway. And he was going to tell Tessa and the girls he was out of the club scene. He would tell them in person tonight. Because he was taking Allie with him. She needed to experience it just once. He figured he knew her well enough that once would be enough.

Later that night, as Allie laughed about their crazy evening of dancing with Tessa, Blake, and Cynthia, Winston said, "You'll have lots of stories to tell your grandkids someday. About the week that you went skydiving, learned to surf, and went clubbing in downtown L.A."

Allie hoped there would be grandchildren someday. For now, there was no use worrying about it. And in the meantime, she was tucking away a pleasant assortment of cherished memories.

Chapter 9

Gary

THERE WAS SOMETHING FISHY about the way it all happened, Gary thought.

How could Alexandria disappear at the precise moment some idiot had knocked him down with a volleyball? And as he replayed the scene in his head, he was positive the guy had purposely blocked his view of Alexandria. The incident was no accident.

He'd tried to tell the police. They'd nodded and sympathized and declared it a horribly tragic coincidence. But Gary didn't believe in coincidences. The whole thing was a plot—a conspiracy. But who did Alexandria know in California that would help her like that? It always came back to that. Somehow, she'd met someone and set this whole thing up. But she didn't have a phone or internet. There was always snail mail, but they lived a long way from the post office, and his wife's time was always accounted for. She had not been in town for a long, long time. The pastor had come to check on her a few times, but she was always out riding or Gary had some excuse that prevented his wife from confiding in the man.

Gary had gone tearfully to his parents, expecting sympathy, help, and understanding. Instead, they questioned him for not taking better care of his wife and yelled at him for ruining their chances of ever having grandchildren. They wanted Gary to cover the deposit they had already paid at the fertility clinic since Alexandria couldn't make the appointment. The echoes of "Can't you ever do anything right?' ricocheted torturously in his head.

He spent most of his "vacation" at the beach where she had disappeared, walking up and down the coastline, searching both water and beach. Often, he would question others he passed trekking across the sand. He called the authorities three times a day. He also called the hospitals. Maybe she was fine but had amnesia.

It was the worst week of his life.

At first, his parents were supportive of the search. At times, he felt they were more desperate to find her than he was. Precious time was ticking, with no hope of grandchildren on the horizon.

Two weeks had passed with no signs and no clues. He had walked up and down the beach so many times his feet hurt. He had asked questions and shown Alexandria's picture to everyone he met.

Gary thought it seemed super unlikely that Alexandria's body hadn't washed up on the beach or been found by fishermen. But when it came to the ocean, the lifeguards and rescue workers had told him regretfully, riptides, sharks, or almost anything could be a factor.

The police told him the trail had gone cold. The only lead they had was that guy Aaron who said he'd thought she was drowning but was too far away to know for sure. He had the description of her right, however. Could he be a part of the conspiracy? Gary wondered. It would be the perfect way to lead him and the police to the wrong conclusions.

When he brought that up to the police, they did investigate. They questioned a lot of Aaron's close friends and family members. They searched Aaron's home. Nothing.

He was out of ideas, and his parents were pressuring him to get back to the ranch.

The police had told him they might wait up to a year before legally declaring her deceased, but for them it was just a formality. They were officially closing the case.

But in his gut, Gary felt Alexandria was not only alive but close by. And if he went back to South Dakota, he would miss his chance to find and reclaim her. He didn't want to return until he knew for sure she was dead.

She was going to wish she were dead if he ever laid his hands on her again, he vowed.

Chapter 10 ──────────────────────────────

A Surprise Visit

WINSTON AND ALLIE WERE eating a light lunch in the dining room when the doorbell rang.

Sebastian came in and cleared his throat. Winston looked up expectantly. "Yes?"

"Sir? Your mother is here," Sebastian announced. The true professional only looked slightly rattled, but Winston was full-blown alarmed. Sebastian shot the briefest of glances in Allie's direction.

Winston had that deer-in-the-headlights look. "What should I tell her about—" He nodded in Allie's direction, to her extreme amusement.

"The truth, sir."

Winston bounded to his feet and swept out of the dining room, heading to the foyer. "Mother! What a pleasant surprise! What brings you to my humble abode this fine day?"

"What you are really thinking is, 'Why didn't you call first?'" she answered in her sophisticated, cultured voice.

If he played it Sebastian's way and told the truth, he would have to answer, "Yes. Why didn't you call first?" But instead of answering, he reached for his mother's hands and kissed her on the cheek. She loved it when he did that. "So good to see you," he said.

"Really?" She didn't sound at all convinced. "Then why do you always have an excuse when I try to come by or set up lunch or something?"

"Because they are not excuses, Mother. They are prior engagements," he answered lightly.

"For someone who doesn't work, rarely studies, and attends very few classes, you seem to have an extremely excessive number of prior engagements," she complained.

"I am rather popular," Winston said in a most charming way.

Grace Grover rolled her eyes.

Sebastian glided toward them. "May I take your jacket, madam? And your purse? Would you like refreshments in the formal living room?"

Sebastian had wisely deferred to Winston's mother for direction, and Winston waited for the answer. She slipped out of her jacket and handed it and her purse to Sebastian, then turned to Winston. "Well, can my popular son spare a few moments for his mother?" she asked. When Winston said yes, she nodded to Sebastian. "Some refreshments would be wonderful."

Winston guiltily realized he hadn't spent time with his mother in months. In fact, it had probably last been on Mother's Day, a holiday he'd felt highly pressured into spending with her. They'd had a lovely luncheon at the country club, where Winston had fought to stay awake and look interested as she prattled on about the garden club awards and how she lost the Most Elegant Garden Award to that awful Judy Cumberland again, who did in fact seem to have the Midas touch with roses. She'd also talked about her golf instructor and how he thought her game had improved immensely in the last year and a half. She'd also talked about how busy her husband was and how she never heard much from Winston's sister, Amanda, who now had a one-year-old and a three-year-old. Amanda lived in New York with her Wall Street–tycoon husband. Her mother hated having her grandchildren and daughter so far away, but she went once a month to visit and had talked nonstop about the babies the entire rest of the luncheon. So, even though Winston's sister lived on the opposite coast—three thousand miles away instead of ten, like Winston—his mother saw her daughter far more regularly than her son.

Pretty pathetic, Winston thought guiltily.

Of course, it had been even longer since he'd had a civil conversation with his father. He certainly hadn't taken his father to lunch at the country club on Father's Day. His avoidance tactics had worked rather remarkably. So maybe last Christmas was when he last saw him? He had to hand it to his father, though. He could turn on the grandfatherly charm when the babies were around. Amanda, with family and nanny in tow, had swept in for the holidays. It was quite the Norman Rockwell scene, Winston thought, with steaming mugs of hot chocolate, presents under the tree, a bright-eyed toddler awed by Christmas lights and ornaments, a mother delighted to have her daughter and little ones home for Christmas, and a father who'd only worked three-quarters of the day on Christmas Eve and had actually taken Christmas Day off.

Winston couldn't remember Christmas being that joyous of an occasion even when he was little. Usually, his grandparents came for a stuffy, formal dinner. Winston and Amanda were forced to abandon their new Christmas delights to participate in the boring dinner with the old people. Dad and Grandfather talked work. Grandmother criticized. Mother was uptight. Winston and Amanda longed to be among their stacks of presents. Winston could not lodge a single complaint in the gift department. He'd always scored well. It was just that the dinners had seemed so long. The minute hand never moved.

The problem last Christmas was Winston had felt completely ignored. His father had asked how law school was progressing, then shook his head in disgust and refused to talk to Winston again.

For Winston, it was better that way. Let his father forget he existed. Then he could keep coasting. His mother was lonely and called Winston quite a bit, but she'd soon gotten the hint and left Winston alone too.

He hadn't needed his parents in years.

But he could use a little help now.

He still hadn't figured out what to do with Allie. His mother wasn't half bad. He hadn't really had any issues with her growing up. It was his father who'd been the strict, cold one. Sadly, he had gradually turned his warm, sociable wife into his clone, but she hadn't always been so cold and formal. What did Winston have to lose? He believed his mother would approve of what Winston had done to rescue Allie, and she might even have some good ideas or knowledgeable connections. At any rate, what would it hurt to take his mother into his confidence? She would probably love it.

And Winston recognized when he was in too deep. He was definitely in too deep.

"Sebastian, could you bring refreshments for three? And have Allie join us? I would like to introduce her to my mother."

Sebastian's wide smile came and went so fast Winston wondered if he had imagined it. "Of course." He bowed and was gone. Winston led his mother into the formal living room and motioned for her to sit in the comfortable wingback.

"Who is Allie?" Grace asked.

Winston was trying to figure how to tell his mother when, to his great relief, Allie walked in.

"Hi," she said shyly. "Sebastian said to join you here?" She looked uncertainly at the elegant older woman whose brow was furrowed in astonishment.

Winston smiled. "Allie Tackleman, meet my mother, Grace Grover."

The woman's jaw dropped. She stared at Allie with wide eyes. "Alexandria Tackleman? The woman on the news who disappeared at the beach and everyone presumed had drowned? You are *that* Allie Tackleman?" Grace answered, her voice shooting up an octave.

Allie and Winston looked at each other. "I'm still in the news?" Allie asked.

Winston looked sheepish. "Yeah, I kind of thought it best not to tell you, but in hindsight, that may have been a mistake," he said.

"So that's why we didn't go out much until recently and you haven't helped me figure out what to do with my life. You've been waiting for the media to move on to the next big story, haven't you?"

"Guilty as charged," Winston said. "Mother, I helped Allie escape from an extremely abusive situation. The situation was so bad we kind of thought it best to make her permanently disappear."

"Your husband wouldn't just grant you a divorce?" Grace asked.

Allie looked at Winston for support and then plunged into her story, not sparing any of the details. Grace looked aghast, then a little sick. And what have I been complaining about all these years? she thought to herself. A hardworking husband who is driven to succeed and determined to give his wife and children the best of everything? She felt a hot flush of remorse creep up her neck. She was horrified this quiet, strong young woman had to endure so much. She was indignant when Allie told her about Gary turning her own mother against her and all the undermining he had accomplished around their town to completely seal her fate and isolate her. Imagine not even having access to a car or telephone. It was unheard of yet smacked of the *Dateline* episodes she'd seen on primetime television.

"And how did you meet Allie and find out about her situation?" Grace asked.

45

Allie and Winston looked at each other again, and Winston nodded at Allie to answer. "I was at the beach. I came to L.A. because Gary's parents wanted us to visit and undergo testing at a fertility clinic. I begged Gary to let me see the ocean. I had never been out of South Dakota. Winston saw me and rescued me. I had been praying earnestly every day for a way out. Your son was the answer to that prayer."

Grace looked wide-eyed at Winston. "And how did you rescue her? How did you know to rescue her?"

"Well, I watched closely for a while. She showed every indication of being abused. At first I tried to ignore the situation. I was about to get some lunch when I had the most intense feeling, this tremendous urge, to help her and to do it right at that moment. I was just planning to help her go for a quick swim, but as I got closer, I could see the bruises all over her body. Dave saw them too. He knocked the guy down, blocked his view, and tried to haul him to first aid. I just quickly escorted Allie to shore, put a large hooded robe on her, and we walked away."

"Incredible," Grace said, shaking her head in wonder. "So now what are you going to do?" she asked.

"I'm not sure. How long should we lie low? And then what do you suggest we do, Mother? I can't think of a situation yet that you haven't been able to handle," Winston said.

Grace could hear the admiration in his voice and felt deeply pleased. Her son had noticed? She thought of how she'd talked her way through his failing grade in seventh-grade English and getting it changed to a C. She thought of how angry the neighbors had been when he'd broken their window with a baseball and they'd threatened to call the police. She could think of a few more scrapes she had helped her son through. And now, years later, she was actually getting some acknowledgment. She was deeply touched and gratified. Her son was turning to her for help. He needed her. It was a wonderful feeling.

"I need to give it some thought," she answered. "Allie, you have my full support. Winston, I want you to know how proud I am of you. Your quick thinking and spontaneous actions saved this lovely young girl."

Allie went over to Grace's chair. "Thank you so much, Mrs. Grover. Could I give you a hug?"

Grace stood uncertainly. A hug? She couldn't remember the last time someone other than her sweet and impulsive young grandchildren had given her a hug. Allie embraced her warmly, erasing Grace's uncertainty and filling her with warmth. Allie whispered in her ear, "Thank you for raising such an amazing son. He truly did save me, and he has been so good to me. I will be forever grateful." She gave her another squeeze.

Grace tried to recall the last time she felt so loved, honored, and important. What a crazy paradigm shift she'd experienced in the last hour. Her worries about the garden club, and what Marilyn was gossiping to all her friends about her behind her back, and feeling neglected by her husband and children, melted in comparison to the problems Allie had experienced. She couldn't imagine being forced to fake your own death to escape a loveless marriage and a man who kept you prisoner and abused you. She thought about her own marriage.

For years, decades even, she had thrown playing second fiddle to Jonathan's work in his face. She had grown cold and distant as a way to punish him. But had she really been punishing herself? She realized she had. She knew Jonathan received a lot of personal fulfillment from work and he assumed she received that same sense of purpose from her children. And for a lot of years, she had. But children had a way of growing up far too quickly. The years of being an empty nester loomed long and lonely. Maybe Jonathan couldn't or wouldn't change. But she could. She made up her mind to start that change without further delay. Life was too short and too uncertain.

Grace sensed Winston's impatience to reach some decisions—even if they were temporary ones. He had been playing the role of perfect host, but she knew he had a life he was likely itching to get back to. She would have been shocked to know that Winston had made up his mind to pass the bar and start practicing law. She thought about the possibilities. Her monthly trip to visit Amanda gave her an idea.

"Would you like to go to New York with me?" she asked.

New York? First L.A. and then New York. Allie's eyes widened in surprise. But Winston brought the whole thing crashing down when he brought up her lack of ID—no driver's license, no birth certificate, no passport. If they got copies of her birth certificate or social security card, it would surely tip off Gary that she was still alive. Yet, if they didn't, how would she ever travel or enroll in school or get a job?

"I'm sorry, Winston. I thought I might be helping solve some problems by hiding her away from the media, but here I am just creating problems," Grace said.

"Not at all, Mother," Winston said. "You just brought them to our attention, and I am glad you did. This is an important step forward in helping her to create a new life for herself. Doesn't Dad have some connections where we can get her birth certificate without tipping her husband off? Then Dad could go through legal channels to help Allie change her name."

"You are right. And I know Allie said that Gary would never divorce her, but I think your father should at least start getting the divorce papers together. It's the only way Allie will ever be free. If Allie gives him everything in the divorce, why wouldn't he want to?"

"Good point. Allie hasn't been able to see things with us in her corner, backing her both financially and legally. She's been worried about it being his word against hers with no witnesses in her behalf, but now she has us. Personally, I think it's a total game changer."

"I agree 100 percent," Grace said.

For now, Allie was stuck. But at least the process for her to start a new life was beginning.

〜 〜

A few days after their original conversation, Grace came over, and they met again in the formal living room.

"I have given this a lot of thought, both the short-term and the long-term," Grace said. "The main long-term goal should be to get a divorce from Gary so that you will be free to marry again if you choose but mainly so you have complete closure and he will no longer have any control or power over you to do you any harm. The other long-term goals are for you to choose, and the short-term goals will lead you there. What is it you really want in life?"

"To be happy, I guess," Allie said.

"And what makes you happy?" Grace asked. "What do you enjoy doing?"

Allie looked at her hands in her lap and was quiet for a long, long time. Finally, she said, "Honestly, just being away from Gary makes me happy. Is that awful of me to say? I did enjoy ranching—being around the cattle and riding my horse and feeling the wind in my face. To some degree, I enjoyed the quiet and solitude, but now that I'm around people a lot—Winston and his friends—I think I'm more social than I realized. So I enjoy being around people. I've been reading a lot. I like learning new things. I've loved having new adventures and new experiences. I have been so happy since I escaped from Gary."

She looked up to see her two friends completely absorbed in her soliloquy. She was so fortunate to have found such a refuge! Before, when she'd thought of escaping, she had pictured herself getting away with the clothes on her back, washing dishes, waitressing, cleaning hotel rooms, and doing anything she could to scrape by and earn enough to feed and house herself. To many, that would seem a miserable existence, especially when compared with the beauty of the ranchland she worked and lived on. But to Allie, it would have been an escape in and of itself. But these good kind souls were offering her so much more. What *did* she really want? Did anyone ever know for sure? Or did it take a lifetime of discovery?

"I think you should go to college," Grace said. "And I think you should live in a dorm or with some roommates. In my opinion, your youth and childhood were ripped away from you. You were robbed of many of the wonderful experiences that come with living on your own for the first time. I feel like you should take classes—maybe some general studies to plug any gaps in your education—but also fun classes, like swimming, pottery, or ballet."

"Ballet?" Allie asked. She pictured graceful ballerinas in pink toe shoes with ribbons wrapped around their ankles and their hair in buns, floating through the air like cotton-candy swans.

"Would you like to try ballet?" Grace asked.

"Sure!" Allie said.

"Winston, bring in your laptop. Let's pull up the class list and see what other things Allie would like to take for her first semester. And then we need to look for apartments near campus so she will be within walking distance."

"I will get my laptop, but I want her to live with Jenna."

"Jenna! What a splendid idea," Grace agreed. "I have always loved and admired that girl. Why did you two not get together?"

"We tried, Mother. We just never meshed. There was always something holding one or the other of us back. I don't know why. But you are right that she is wonderful. And I can't think of anyone I would trust more to take care of Allie right now," Winston said.

"I agree," Grace said, looking pleased. "Let's call her right away and see if she can make room for Allie in her apartment. Isn't the semester due to start next week?"

Winston was already reaching into his pocket for his cell phone. "Jenna? It's Winston. I've got a favor to ask ..."

Chapter 11 ———————————————————

Roommates

LOOKING BACK FROM THE wisdom of a couple of years, Jenna could tell she had sabotaged the relationship. She knew she was unlike any of the other girls Winston had dated, and she had concluded she wasn't good enough.

Hindsight was always twenty-twenty.

With perfect clarity, she could see how she'd set the relationship up for failure because, in her heart, she had known it was doomed. She wasn't pretty enough. She wasn't intelligent enough. She wasn't athletic enough. And since she didn't come from money, she had no idea about the social graces that came with having money.

She still cringed thinking about the time Winston took her to the country club. They had golfed nine holes already, and Winston, always the gentleman, had sensed her fatigue.

"Why don't we go have some lunch, and we will see whether or not we want to play the other nine holes?"

Jenna agreed, although she was constantly intimidated by the stream of wealthy, sophisticated people who stopped by their table to chat with Winston and ask about his family. Winston always politely introduced Jenna, but she was always tongue-tied.

The mortifying moment came when a group of four older gentlemen approached their table, greeted them, and then asked, "And what's your handicap?"

"My handicap?" Jenna had choked out, turning red.

They'd all looked at her with surprise and raised eyebrows. No one knew what to say. Winston had tried to ease the awkward moment, saying, "She's too new to the golfing scene to establish one."

The men had moved off, some chuckling. Jenna had wanted to slip through a wormhole to the other side of the universe. She couldn't seem to stop herself from saying stupid things or seemingly expecting the worst from Winston, even though Winston constantly proved otherwise. Maybe it was because of his revolving door of prior girlfriends, maybe it was partying with Tessa and his two other wild friends, she thought with guilt and red-faced shame over her harsh judgment. She just couldn't get past her own insecurity and give the relationship a chance.

It was a real shame too. Winston was everything a woman would want in a man, and she'd blown it. The final straw had come when he'd asked her to go to his sister's wedding as his date. She'd picked out an elegant, long, red satin dress and looked the part, even if she didn't feel it. She'd had a couple of drinks and apparently told a couple of people she had no idea why Winston would date her. That would have been bad enough. But when they were dancing, he'd spun her around. The combination of being a bit drunk and off-balance in conjunction with being unused to such high heels and long dresses led to disaster. She'd toppled on one stiletto, reached out a hand to steady herself, skidded on the hem of her satin dress, and caught her fall with the help of the $2,000 seven-tiered wedding cake.

The entire wedding party seemed to turn like synchronized swimmers and collectively gasped. Jenna was glad that at least the cake had covered her face as she ran out. The cake was utterly ruined.

Forever after, her relationship with Winston was also utterly ruined. Winston had tried to convince her that no one cared. Accidents happened. His sister laughed it off. Even her mother had forgiven her. But Jenna could never face them again. She would rather give up this perfect, kind, handsome man than be forced into uncomfortable social situations time after time.

And so she had buried herself in college life, with a laser-like focus on getting her degree and life on track.

If only she could take Social Graces 101 . . .

༄ ༄

Winston understood what she was going through to some degree. Though he himself never felt out of his social element, he was usually sensitive to what others were thinking and feeling, and there was always this under-current of uncertainty and inadequacy when he was dating Jenna that just seemed to knock their entire relationship off-kilter.

Winston blamed himself for not being good enough or encouraging enough to give Jenna the self-confidence she needed to succeed. He wasn't used to failure, but he felt like he'd completely failed Jenna. Maybe that's why he couldn't completely give up on the relationship. He felt he still owed her something.

And yet, here he was, outside her door because he had asked her for a favor. Allie stood nervously beside him, shifting from foot to foot. Winston grinned at her. "Nothing to worry about. Jenna is the best," he told her.

"What if they don't like me?" she asked.

"Why wouldn't they like you?" Winston asked, surprised. He would never get women, nor would he even want to. "Besides, it doesn't matter. If for some crazy reason they don't like you, there are millions of others who will, and we can find someone for you to live with at college. And if you don't like them, same plan. We just find you new roommates. And if you really can't find anyone you can stand to live with," Winston chuckled, "then welcome to college-roommate life."

Allie winced. "Is it really that bad?"

"I'm mostly kidding," he answered. "But if there really isn't anyone you want to live with, there is always me. I'm your safety net, your friend. I'm here for the long-term. I didn't just walk into your life and pluck you out of a bad situation in order to leave you."

Allie was hugging him when the door flew open. Allie couldn't have been more surprised. Having met Elizabeth, Tessa, and the other women that Winston hung out with and knowing that he'd once dated Jenna, she'd pictured another perfectly put-together, long-legged model with long, sleek hair straight from a Paul Mitchell commercial. The woman who opened the door was dressed in a UCLA sweatshirt splattered with paint. She even had paint on her face but no makeup. Her high ponytail bounced. She looked about sixteen, although Allie knew she had to be much older if she was a senior in college.

She was invited inside the apartment and swooped upon by a couple of other girls, who gave her a hug.

"Hi! You're here!"

Then they rushed over to hug Winston. "We've missed you, Winston!"

"We've been waiting for you to come! We are so excited!"

Katie was so vivacious that both Allie and Winston broke into wide grins. They were ushered to comfy chairs, and Allie was introduced and hugged again and welcomed all around.

He hoped Allie was really going to like her new roommates.

Katie was bright, athletic, fun, and the social butterfly of every function. She stood out in class. The guys asked her for study "help" but really just wanted to take her out. They would talk about class for a while and then drop the pretense and take her to dinner, a party, an escape room, or whatever. The same thing happened at the gym. She would be lifting weights or on a bike and some guy would come over to "help" her. He would have secretly been admiring her from a distance. They would work out together for a while, and then he would ask her out. Katie didn't really play favorites. Whichever guy wanted to help her or take her out to dinner was her best friend.

Winston liked Katie, and Katie liked Winston. But he was too unsettled, too flighty, too selfish, too undisciplined for her. Happily, they shared a comfortable friendship.

Sailor was a little shyer, more uncertain, and a fairly new roommate, but she was also just as friendly and kindhearted as Katie. She watched and observed, content to be in the background. And she learned a lot from Jenna and Katie.

Later, when Allie was in the other room laughing with Katie, Winston said, "I'm so glad they've hit it off."

Jenna looked at him. "She is a wonderful woman, a fighter with such a great attitude, but she sounds like a prisoner of war."

"In a way, she was," Winston said. "I think you three will be just what she needs. You will provide support, friendship, encouragement, and fun. You will give her a chance to see what life is really about."

"I will do my best to take good care of her," Jenna said.

Winston clasped her hand. "I know. That's why I'm here. She needs you. She needs your kindness, intelligence, and guidance. But I hope you don't feel like I am dumping her on you. If it doesn't work out, please let me know. I have thought long and hard about what might be best for her as she moves ahead in a new life."

"I'm touched, Winston, by your faith in me. And I genuinely already like her. I will let you know if it doesn't work out for some reason, but I have a really good feeling about it."

Winston grinned at her. "So do I."

Right on cue, more laughter came from the other room.

Chapter 12 ——————————————————————————————

Dad Finds Out

JONATHAN GROVER COULDN'T BELIEVE his ears. Was his wife really telling him the missing woman from the news was living at their son's house? He couldn't comprehend it. But what else was new? He basically couldn't comprehend anything his son did. His entire lifestyle was a mystery. Why would you want to lie around the beach or even take up surfing when you could be developing a successful career? What was the appeal of making the rounds in the horrible dating scene when, obviously, Winston could snatch up Miss America if he wanted to, experience wedded bliss, and raise a family of his own? And how could he stand to live on his father's handouts when he was fully capable of providing for himself?

When Jonathan turned eighteen, he could barely tolerate his own father paying his college tuition and expenses. Jonathan would have preferred student loans and minuscule studio apartments rather than owe his father anything. He wanted to be a self-made man. Well, he'd proven over and over that he was just that. Winston just left him scratching his head.

Now this.

"And so what do you want *me* to do?" he asked his wife.

"We were hoping you'd be willing to draft up some divorce papers," Grace said.

"I thought you said the husband will not agree to a divorce," he said.

Grace nodded. "True. And as it stands, he doesn't know she is alive. Allie is presumed dead. We also were hoping for your assistance with getting her some new identification: a driver's license, social security card, and even a passport, but we don't want to alert her husband to the fact that she is alive and living in California."

Jonathan ran his hands roughly down his face. What a nightmare. And now Winston was trying to drag him into the middle of it? He was about to decline when he looked at his wife's face. Grace looked so hopeful. So involved. Happy, even.

When was the last time his wife had come into the city and to his office and asked for anything? He couldn't remember when it was, but he could remember the specific details and how he had handled it. He felt shame-faced still. She had looked beautiful that day. He had burst with pride as his wife warmly greeted the receptionist and talked to his partner with ease. Her hair was perfect, her nails were perfect—everything about her was perfect. She had asked him to go to lunch. He was right in the middle of a case about to go to trial, but he thought he might be able to spare a few minutes for a quick lunch. Grace waited patiently. Maybe too patiently because he forgot all about her. Two hours later, she came back into his office, asking if he would be ready for lunch soon. She wasn't angry or snappish, she just wanted to know. Jonathan was the one who became angry and snappish.

"You're still, here?" he'd asked impatiently. "What was it you wanted—well, other than going to lunch?"

Grace had looked a little embarrassed. Jonathan could always see right through her. She felt guilty she had an ulterior motive. She looked up at him, unsure whether or not this was the time to ask. But, for once, his full attention was on her.

"I did have something important I wanted to ask you," she said quietly.

He'd silently waited for her to continue.

"Jonathan, you know I have been volunteering at the hospital."

He'd nodded.

"Well, recently, there was a family who was in a devastating car crash. The father was killed immediately, as were the two youngest children. The mother and oldest child, a nine-year-old girl, were both in serious condition when they came in, and both underwent immediate surgery."

Jonathan patiently watched her as she spoke, not interrupting but confused as to where this conversation was leading. Maybe she hoped he would cover their medical bills.

"The little girl suffered a lot of internal bleeding and some broken bones, but she is recovering. The mother, however, suffered significantly more trauma and passed away yesterday." A tear formed at the corner of Grace's eye and slowly slid down her cheek.

Jonathan wanted to reach out and hold her, but he held back. "I'm so sorry. That must be the hardest part about volunteering at the hospital— seeing such horrible things happen to nice families," he said with sympathy.

Grace nodded and looked at him steadily. "Jonathan, I would like to adopt that little girl. She is an orphan now. I have talked with her, and she is very sweet."

Stunned, Jonathan shook his head. "I'm sorry, but I don't think that is a good idea."

"Why not?"

"Because of our age. I have colleagues younger than I am who have nine-year-old grandchildren. Do you realize how old we would be when she graduates from college? What if our health deteriorates and we can't take care of her? That would force Amanda to take care of her or, heaven forbid, Winston. We could be making a commitment our children might be forced to follow up on."

"No one knows what the future holds. Look what happened to this poor family! Plus, if something happened to us, she would have the money to be provided for. Amanda and Winston may not have to be involved. But by then, I would hope they would accept her as their sister and want to take care of her," Grace argued.

"I don't think so, Grace. Our own two children are still not settled. Who knows where Amanda and Winston will end up? And I'm getting close to the point where I might want to retire. I'm thinking of Europe, the Mediterranean, New Zealand, and all the places we have talked about see- ing. Can you picture dragging a teenager around with us?"

He could tell Grace had no problem picturing it, actually.

They'd argued and argued. Grace had cried and begged, but Jonathan wouldn't budge. All along, both of them knew it was Jonathan who held the power. He was never easily persuaded to do anything. Why on earth had Grace pictured him capitulating to a monumental life change?

And now, here she was again, trying to "adopt" another girl. Part of him admired Grace for her soft, caring heart. But mostly he felt irritation. Couldn't she just be happy with her situation? Didn't she have absolutely everything?

Still, he carried the guilt of having said no to her all those years ago. Truly, she had tried not to hold a grudge. But she always looked at children when there were any around to look at. And she had never volunteered at the hospital again.

He sighed.

"Ok. I will look into it," he said, a bit defeated.

Grace came up to him and kissed him warmly. "Thank you," she whispered, and with a twinkle in her eye, she added, "Would you like to take me to lunch?"

Chapter 13 ───────────────────────────

College

ALLIE COULD NOT STOP the fluttering in her stomach. Today, she became a college student. The thought made her simultaneously want to do backflips and throw up.

Winston had helped her to enroll in several classes. She couldn't decide which one she most looked forward to. She had a literature class, and she loved to read. For her science class, Winston had suggested she study earth science, another subject she was both interested in and already quite familiar with. For some math credits, he suggested she take a life-skills, real-world math application class and then maybe next time she could attempt algebra, a subject she had never had the opportunity to try. Picking a history class proved to be the most difficult. She wanted to know everything about everything! So she decided to start at the beginning—with the history of ancient civilizations. With twelve difficult credits, Winston suggested she add one or two one-credit classes for fun. So with great joy, she signed up for ballet and a swim class.

"Perfect," Winston had declared. He was almost as thrilled about the schedule as Allie was, which Allie thought adorable.

Winston's father had come through with identification, and Allie was officially enrolled. To be going back to school after dropping out of the eighth grade was daunting but exciting. She couldn't stop the trembling in her hands.

"Ready?" Jenna asked, giving her hand a squeeze.

Jenna had been everything Winston said and more. Jenna had become Allie's rock as, once again, she transitioned into a new life. She couldn't believe how much fun "girl talk" was. Katie and Sailor were bubbly and out-going, whereas Jenna and Allie were more serious and reserved. But each of them was adept at drawing Allie more and more out of her shell. Winston had been astounded by the changes in her after just one week.

"Whoa! You're suddenly acting like a college co-ed!" he'd said.

Allie had just grinned at the compliment. Now she was off, slinging a nondescript backpack in a stylish simulation of Sailor. Besides her designer clothes, Allie had cut and highlighted her hair to a California blonde to enhance her disguise. Even Grace was confident that not even the most avid news watcher would recognize her from her picture.

Jenna dropped her off near her class. Feeling like a kindergartener who wished her mom could sit next to her on the first day, she walked into the classroom, nervously tucking a strand of hair behind her ear as she perused the room. A smattering of students was already seated, most hunched over cell phones, scrolling mindlessly. She turned her attention to the professor, who was also discreetly assessing each of the students. Allie made eye contact and smiled. Winston would be so proud of her!

Between Jenna and Winston, she had had a lot of coaching and prac-tice with being around other people again. Instead of being intimidated, she found it empowering. She was through with cowering. Why had she handed all the power over to Gary, anyway? The situation was completely different, she reminded herself. He had turned her own mother against her, and she'd had no one to turn to. Well, now that she did, things were going to be different.

A man hustled in just as class was about to start and smiled at her as he slipped into the seat in front of her. The professor stood and welcomed them to her literature class, then introduced a wide selection of genres, in-cluding dystopian, fantasy, and both old and modern classics. They were going to start with *Fahrenheit 451*. Allie had never heard of it, but the man in front of her was nodding. Professor Garrett talked about the author, Ray Bradbury, and some of his other works and then about other books in the dystopian genre, also recommending *Brave New World*. Allie could feel her excitement building. She couldn't wait to start reading.

Winston had given her a $1,000 monthly allowance, so she planned to head directly to the bookstore and purchase all of the books in Professor Garrett's syllabus. When class ended, she gathered her backpack. Maybe she would ask the professor how to get to the bookstore. Why hadn't she asked Jenna to give her a tour of campus?

"Have you read *Fahrenheit 451* before?" the man in front of her asked, coming to his feet.

Allie shook her head. "No, I'm just heading to the bookstore to buy it—if I can find the bookstore," she said offhandedly. "Have you read it?"

"I have. It's fantastic. A great choice. This particular genre is a favorite of mine, and I've read quite extensively in it. I've heard Professor Garrett is one of the best. I've been looking forward to taking this class. By the way," he said, extending his hand, "I'm Daniel. Daniel Munroe. I am also heading to the bookstore. Would you mind terribly if I went with you?"

"Mind?" Allie laughed. "I would be grateful for your help in getting there."

"So are you a new transfer? Where are you from?"

"I'm a freshman, actually." Winston had told her to just tell the truth about herself, but, of course, also keep the private things private. Oh, how she loved advice from that man! "And I'm from South Dakota. How about you?"

"I am from Arizona—Scottsdale, to be exact. My family tried to get out of the scorching summer heat as much as possible, so I've spent a lot of time in California. I've had my eye on this university for a long time. You say you are a freshman from South Dakota? I want to hear more."

He looked so sincere that Allie felt herself warming to him. "I grew up on a cattle ranch. I spent more time feeding cattle and fixing fences than reading, I'm afraid. I do love to read, though," she said, trying to steer the conversation back to the safety of books.

"Well, you are in the right class, then," he said. "What other classes are you taking?"

Allie told him her other classes. He nodded politely. "What do you plan to major in?" he asked.

Allie grinned. "I have no idea."

"Ah! A true freshman," he said, nodding. "You've got plenty of time to decide, and I think you have some very well-rounded choices on the docket."

"Thanks! How about you? What year, and what is your major?"

"I'm a senior studying structural engineering."

They talked so easily and pleasantly Allie was sad when they reached the bookstore. She figured Daniel would be happy to be rid of her and go his way. She would, however, have the pleasure of seeing him Mondays, Wednesdays, and Fridays. She hoped he continued to sit in the desk in front of her.

"Could I help you find your book, and then would you like to go have a cup of coffee?" he surprised her by asking.

"That would be wonderful," she agreed.

She couldn't stop smiling. The professor was wonderful. The campus was wonderful. Daniel was wonderful. She had money to buy books she was itching to read. This cute guy was helping her and had asked her to coffee. She could already hear the screaming from her three roommates about her triumphant debut.

They did not disappoint.

"Woot! Woot!"

"Go, Allie!"

"Tell me more about this guy! Daniel, did you say?"

"I never had a first day like that," Sailor complained, crossing her arms.

"Who has?" Jenna agreed.

"I think it's just because I'm older," Allie said. "The combination of being older yet inexperienced was ..."

"Irresistible!" Sailor said, laughing. They all joined in.

"He was very nice—the kind of guy who would take care of a bird with a broken wing or climb a tree to rescue a scared kitten. I probably had that lost look and he wanted to rescue me as well. I told him I didn't know where the bookstore was, and he must have felt obligated to help me get there," Allie said.

Her roommates smiled. "He sounds wonderful. You should bring him over," Katie said.

"What I really need to do is warn him that I'm married," Allie said, deflated.

"I wish we could get that taken care of so you're not married," Jenna said. The roommates knew all of the details and promised it would only come up inside their apartment.

"How about if I say I'm in a long-distance relationship?" Allie asked. "That I have someone back in South Dakota."

"Genius. Then you are being honest with him while keeping the door to friendship open. I can tell you are interested in him, and by the sound of it, he is definitely into you," Jenna exclaimed.

Allie felt a rush of warmth. So many friends and so many nice people kept coming into her life. It was overwhelming but wonderful. And Daniel felt like such a loyal, wonderful person to have in her corner. But it got her thinking about what she had always pushed to the back of her mind. What if she was not able to have children?

She had been able to confide her most personal hopes and fears with Jenna. It was an uncomfortable topic, but she couldn't think of a better person to turn to. She finally got up the courage to ask.

Allie turned with troubled eyes to her friend. "During my marriage, I thought it was a miracle I never got pregnant. But now I'm worried. What if I can't have children?"

"How long were you married?" Jenna asked.

"Five years. So maybe something is medically wrong with me and I will never have children."

After a pause, Jenna said, "Were you always stressed out in your marriage? On edge?"

"Oh yes. I lived in fear."

"I often hear of married couples who go to an infertility clinic, but it turns out they were just so uptight and feeling pressure to start their family right away that it couldn't happen until they relaxed," Jenna said. "Knowing your situation, I would say with absolute confidence that you would have been uptight and felt a lot of pressure, and that could be why you didn't get pregnant."

Allie looked at Jenna with hopeful eyes. She felt strongly that what Jenna said was true. "That would be wonderful. I would really love to have children someday." She hugged Jenna. "Thank you, Jenna. It's so nice to have friends. And I couldn't have asked for a better friend than you."

Chapter 14

Checking on Allie

WINSTON WAS STUNNED BY the changes in Allie.

When he first met her, she was thin. She had tan skin, but it was marred by smudges and bruising. She had a natural beauty, even without makeup, but her hair had been lifeless, her demeanor dejected. Now, just a couple of weeks into her college classes, she looked vibrant, just like when he took her skydiving and surfing. She had also filled out a little. Her skin tone had mellowed into a rosy shade. She still wore little makeup, but what she did wear enhanced the beauty of her eyes and drew attention to shapely lips.

"You look fantastic," he said, smiling at her. "I have missed you. I want to hear all about how things are going. How do you like college? Your roommates? And, tell me, is every man on campus asking you out on a date, or are they all a bunch of idiots?"

She giggled. "I have had a few guys ask me out, but what am I supposed to do? I'm a married woman. I turn most of them down."

"Most?" Winston laughed. "So you only go out with the best looking of the bunch?"

"No." How to explain? She looked up at the ceiling, then said, "So there is this one guy, Daniel. He became my friend first. Then it just became a natural next step to go on a date. It didn't really feel like a date, though. First, we just went out for coffee. Then we studied together. Then we went to a football game. So, technically, I feel like I am going on dates with him, and yet I also feel like we are just hanging out as friends. I never felt like he

64

officially asked me out, so I didn't really feel like I had to turn him down. Does that make any sense?"

Winston nodded. Smooth operator. "And have you told him you are married?" he asked.

Allie turned scarlet and shook her head. "No. Should I?"

"I'm not sure." Winston pulled at his chin, mulling it over. "On one hand, I really like that you have a man around for protection because I can't be there at school with you. But I also feel like the fewer people who know about your situation, the better. What if he got really angry and somehow found a way to contact your ex?"

Allie shivered. Her eyes went wide with fear. "That would be awful. I can see how I need to be extremely careful about who I trust with my story." Then her eyes softened. "'But Daniel is really kind. I don't think he would ever do that."

"I'm glad to hear that. If you feel like he can be trusted, then I think it is appropriate to tell him your background. Especially if you are just friends. If he has romantic notions, he may be pretty crushed to learn that you're married."

"Well, hopefully, I won't be married for long. I have a lot of faith in your father."

Winston smiled. He had a lot of faith in his father too. And for the first time in a decade, the word *father* made him smile rather than cringe.

"What?" she asked.

"Oh, I am getting along a lot better with my father these days. Thanks to you, Allie."

She smiled at the look of satisfaction, contentment, and happiness radiating from Winston. The listlessness, lack of purpose, and dissatisfaction seemed to have dissipated. "What did I do? I don't think I deserve any credit. But there *is* a change in you, Winston. You are happier. I guess you needed to fix your relationship with your father more than you realized."

"I sure did. What I really needed to do was get my life on track and find a purpose. And you do deserve a lot of the credit. My mom is also happier because of you. You gave us the perspective on life that we needed. She loved being able to help you, and working with my father on that has brought them closer. My father has softened. He quit grilling me about finishing law school. I told you I had stalled out on my final semester, didn't I? I was just big-time dragging my feet because I didn't want to face the next step: taking my place in my father and grandfather's law firm. I felt like I would be chained to it for the rest of my life, like they are. Well, when I finally started studying for the bar, do you know what? I like it. I like studying law. The days just seem to fly by. I feel challenged. I feel alive! I understand my father for the first time in my life. And I feel a connection with him. And you know what it all started with?"

"What?" Allie said, feeling breathless.

"With you coming into my life. Your example. It's made all the difference somehow."

They smiled at each other, and Allie impulsively reached out and hugged him. Winston felt warm in a way that was foreign to him. He chuckled uncomfortably. Sharing his feelings was something he did, like, never.

"So, tell me more about your classes," he said, happy to change the subject. "Which one is your favorite?"

Chapter 15 ————————————————————————

Introductions

"Jenna, this is Daniel. Daniel, this is Jenna." Allie smiled and gestured dramatically to each of them. She had talked about Jenna a lot to Daniel and vice versa, and now that she felt so comfortable with Daniel, she was excited to invite him over.

"Nice to meet you," Jenna said, eyes bright with approval. She closed an enormous textbook and tossed it onto a pile of books on the coffee table and stood up.

"And you," Daniel said, giving her a glance, a warm smile, and a handshake before turning away. He only had eyes for Allie, watching her as she went into the kitchen to get them all some lemonade.

"So, Allie tells me that you have a literature class together and that you especially like dystopian fiction. I really enjoyed the Divergent series," Jenna said, sitting back on the sofa and motioning for Daniel to join her. "And I always loved *Brave New World* and haven't found a book in that genre to match it"

Daniel's eyes widened. "Really? It's good to find another fan. What did you like best about it?" He settled in, happy to talk about one of his favorite subjects.

"The world-building is so realistic it's like I've been transported to a different dimension when I'm reading it. I'm tense and at the same time completely intrigued."

Daniel shifted so that he was leaning closer to Jenna. "That's how I feel when I read dystopian fiction. I throw myself into a fascinating alternate reality."

"Have you ever thought about writing one? In that genre specifically?"

Daniel nodded earnestly. "I actually have a lot of ideas rolling around in my head. I keep trying to push them away so I can concentrate on my studies, though."

"I would love to hear your ideas sometime," Jenna said as Allie entered the room carrying some tall glasses on a tray and passing them around.

"What are you studying?" Daniel asked Jenna.

"I've changed my major a lot," Jenna said, laughing. "But right now, I'm really close to getting a bachelor's degree in social work. I plan to get a master's in psychology."

"Congratulations! You are at least a semester ahead of me," Daniel said. He turned to Allie. "Ready to study? If I can ace this class, I only have five other classes to worry about."

Allie laughed. "Then we better get to it."

Jenna got up, carrying her half-finished lemonade. "Good luck, you two. I'm sure you will both do great. Daniel, it was a pleasure to meet you." Her voice faltered and she sounded uncertain, as she added, "And I hope to hear your ideas one of these days."

"It was nice to meet you too, Jenna," Daniel answered. "If you are really up for it, I would love to test out a few ideas on you."

Jenna smiled and walked out of the room. Oh my! What just happened? she wondered. Daniel was wonderful. He was amazing. He was good-looking, he had been kind to Allie, he was smart, and he shared her penchant for fiction. Why did Allie have to meet him first? The cardinal rule for roommates was no stealing each other's boyfriends, but if your roommate was married, was that rule null and void? Plus, it wasn't fair that Allie had a husband *and* both Winston and Daniel interested in her. Not fair at all.

But she had to admit it wasn't fair that Gary had been so abusive and that he had turned her own mother against her. She might as well face it. Life wasn't fair. But then she smiled again as she thought of Daniel's promise. He would share his ideas with her. She would see it through. And the thought of spending some time with him thrilled her.

∽ ∾

Daniel became a regular visitor to the apartment.

The next time he came, he got to meet Katie and Sailor, and he and Jenna talked easily. Jenna was pleased that in addition to literature, they shared more common interests. They both loved dogs, art, history, and going for walks.

Daniel had all the roommates laughing as he told a story about his dog getting loose and digging up a bone in the yard of a neighbor who had a nippy little dog. The dog was absolutely indignant.

"I can just picture it," Jenna said, gripping her stomach as she laughed. She told him about her favorite childhood dog and her heartbreak when the family had to put the dog down because she was suffering from a tumor. They didn't realize the others had left the room.

"That's the hardest thing ever," Daniel sympathized, "losing a beloved pet like that."

Allie entered the room and was surprised at the connection she sensed between Jenna and Daniel. *Hmm . . . Jenna and Daniel*, she mused.

"I forgot something I need to grab from my room," she said when they both turned to stare at her. She had barely whirled around when they continued their conversation, and she smiled to herself. For now, she was going to study in her room. When, or, perhaps, if, they noticed she was gone or they needed her, they could come find her.

Chapter 16

Studying for the Bar

Whether it was good DNA, his ability to absorb the law over the years, common sense, or a good memory, Winston had retained a lot of what he'd learned throughout law school.

He made up his mind to buckle down and study. When he thought of Allie doing the same thing, he was inspired to keep with it.

His father called to see if everything had worked out with Allie's identification and how she was adjusting to college. Winston was pleased. He was itching to tell his father how close he was to taking the bar exam. Usually, his father gave him the third degree about it when he called. But not this time. Winston was grateful. Maybe the man wasn't so bad after all.

Winston laughed, delighted with his secret. He knew Allie figured he couldn't wait to get back to his normal life of fun now that he didn't have to worry about her. Instead, he had never worked harder in his life. Even Sebastian was shocked.

Weeks blended into months as he studied. He called often to check on Allie. Sometimes he talked to Jenna. Allie was doing great and loving school. She went out to eat or to movies or to other apartments with Sailor and Jenna and Katie or Daniel, but she was also working hard on her studies.

Every time he hung up the phone or came home from a visit with Allie, he felt the deepest happiest sense of satisfaction. Allie was thriving. She was learning and growing and enjoying hanging out with friends. She was eating pizza and Ramen noodles and hauling a backpack around campus.

She was living.

Winston laughed, thinking that Allie had more of a social life than he did. She would probably faint if she knew he stayed home on weekends studying. And weeknights. Every single night.

He passed the bar exam with flying colors.

Finally.

Now, to surprise his father with the news. He hoped this would make all the hard work he had been putting in worth it.

But, first, there was something important he had put off for far too long.

Chapter 17 ————————————————————

Break Up

"Winston, why haven't I heard from you lately?" whined Elizabeth.

"I've been studying nonstop for the bar, Elizabeth, remember?"

"You've been studying for the bar ever since I've known you. It's never cramped our style before. I've missed you. But you did finally pass, didn't you? So can we please go to dinner tomorrow night? I'm really hoping to try that new place downtown everyone is raving about. You've got to eat, don't you?"

Winston agreed that he did have to eat, but the prospect of sharing a meal with Elizabeth made him lose his appetite. Why had he ever thought her attractive? Ok, he did know why. The woman was a drop-dead gorgeous, long-legged model who had every man staring when she walked through a door. Then they would shoot Winston a look of pure jealousy. Winston loved those looks. He craved those looks.

At least he used to.

Now, most of his thoughts swirled around ethics, rights, laws, and justice. And when he allowed himself the chance, his thoughts went to Allie. Whenever he felt down or discouraged, he thought of her smile. He thought of how he felt when he rescued her. He thought of how he felt when they'd surfed together. He thought of how his parents had come together with purpose and how it had been the strongest their marriage had been in years. He thought how Allie had inspired him to pass the bar. Every single thought he had of Allie made him happy.

It was pretty sad that his happy memories of Elizabeth were when other men were jealous of him. He tried to think of happy times with Elizabeth. There was that time they attended the movie premiere and got to walk down the red carpet. Elizabeth had knocked everyone's socks off with her sophisticated, shimmery, Vera Wang, off-the-shoulder gown and matching shimmery shoes reminiscent of Cinderella.

Cameras flashed as the couple smiled. Winston had felt a swell of happiness as he'd intertwined his fingers with Elizabeth's and smiled at her appreciatively, communicating his gratitude for being her date that evening. The movie was an action-packed Daniel Craig James Bond movie that had the audience gasping and cheering.

It was a good memory, he thought. But then he realized it hadn't actually involved any interaction with her. Once again, it was people being envious of him for having his pictures snapped on the red carpet with model Elizabeth Thorpley.

"Winston? Hello, earth to Winston," Elizabeth said, Winston felt more irritated with her. He hadn't heard those obnoxious words since second grade.

"Sorry, I was just remembering that James Bond movie premiere. Remember that?"

"Of course. I wore a Vera Wang and Giovanni shoes and had a Coach clutch," she answered quickly.

Winston paused, waiting to see if he would be included in that memory. But, apparently, that was it, because her next words were, "Are you there? What's your deal today? What time would you like to dine at Delano's?"

Winston could not think of a good excuse, especially given such a flexible timeframe. He should be hungry by seven thirty or eight and hastily told her so before she could berate him some more. Winston hung up and groaned.

Sebastian cleared his throat.

Winston knew Sebastian was dying to say something but didn't want to overstep his boundaries or break "the butler code," as he called it. Winston was pretty sure what he wanted to say, and since he agreed wholeheartedly, he wanted to give him the chance to say it.

"Something on your mind, Sebastian? I'd be happy to hear it," Winston offered.

"Sir, it seems to me that now, more than ever, might be a prudent time to terminate a relationship with a certain beautiful model," he said, looking steadily at his employer.

"I agree that though it was fine while it lasted—not good, but fine—now would be as good a time as any to put an end to the misery."

Sebastian's eyebrows quirked up. "Misery, huh? So you definitely were not in need of my advice," he said.

"On the contrary," Winston countered. "I need it more than ever."

"What do you mean, sir?" Now Sebastian looked puzzled. Winston knew he saw things in black or white so if Winston didn't like the woman, he could just inform her that she could do way better and not waste her time on him. He smiled to himself, knowing that in Sebastian's opinion, of course, it was the other way around but he wanted to be diplomatic about the whole thing.

"Here's the situation, Sebastian. No matter what I say or how gently I do it, I can't break up with her because I will be making an enemy for life. It's got to be her idea. She has to break up with me. I've actually been trying to tick her off in the hopes that she will end the relationship." Winston twirled a pen, concentrating deeply on a plan.

Sebastian nodded. "But you can't anger her too significantly, or you will still invoke her lasting wrath," he agreed. "What is most important to her?"

"Looking good," Winston answered automatically. Then they looked at each other.

That night, Winston decided to hire a limousine for his date with Elizabeth. Might as well start off in her good graces. She would love being seen in a limo. But Winston's main reason for hiring the limousine was for the driver who came with it. As they pulled up to Elizabeth's impressive gated estate, he instructed the driver to please fetch his date.

Elizabeth's nose crunched distastefully when she first opened the door to see an unfamiliar face in a uniform, of all things, then broke into a welcoming smile as she realized the man was her chauffeur for the evening. She gladly took his arm as he escorted her down the elegant wide stone steps to the waiting limo.

The interior of the car stayed dim as Elizabeth ducked into the limo in a swirl of silk and perfume.

"Good evening, Elizabeth," Winston greeted formally. "You are looking lovely as always. How have things been going for you?"

She scooted over to him and gave him a peck on the cheek. "Great! I've landed a new account with Estée Lauder that will plaster my face on advertisements coast to coast."

Winston could see her smiling, her teeth a dazzling white in the gloom. "So we are celebrating, then," Winston said. "How wonderful. Congratulations!"

"Thank you. Unfortunately, they hired some upstart from Paris for their European campaign, so mine will just be on a national level."

This was already so tedious. Why hadn't he found a way to end this long ago? He had been putting her off ever since he had met Allie. Because ever since he had met Allie, he had seen the stark contrast between the two women. Allie was so real. Elizabeth was so fake. Allie was fun to talk to, perhaps because she was so appreciative and compassionate and had such a depth of character. Allie also found a way to be interested in others. Winston had grown tired of hearing all about Elizabeth. The worst was when she complained about her rivals.

Winston decided to change the subject rather than take the bait about the Paris model. "So, were you surprised I hired a limo for the evening?"

"I don't know about surprised, but I think this will draw more attention to us than either your Maserati or Porsche would have." Elizabeth was always selfish with her compliments.

When they pulled up to Delano's, necks craned both inside the restaurant and out as pedestrians and drivers and diners all strained to get a better look at who was coming out of the limousine. If they were hoping for a famous actor or actress, they were going to be disappointed. But Elizabeth wouldn't notice or care about their disappointment. She would only care about the attention fully placed on her and about looking her very best when it happened.

She didn't even look back at Winston as he exited the limo. He just trailed in her wake. Finally, she grabbed his arm, and they entered the restaurant together. It wasn't until they were seated that she actually looked at him for the first time.

She gasped. "Winston! What? What are you wearing?" she asked, horrified.

Winston just smiled. "I wanted all the attention to be on you tonight. So I'm just blending into the woodwork."

"Um, not quite," Elizabeth said, scrunching her nose like she smelled rotted fish. "Seriously, what has gotten into you?"

"This is my new look," Winston said, "I haven't seen you in forever. But I'm about to become a working man, so I decided to start dressing like one."

"All the lawyers, at least the prestigious lawyers I know, they all look *good*," she emphasized. "But you . . ." Her words trailed off. "Won't you work for your father? He's a working man and always dresses in style."

"I've procrastinated for so long I don't know if he will hire me at this point," Winston said, knowing the first part was true but hoping the second part was not. "I might have to start at the bottom. Plus, I have been so busy studying I've hardly left the house and haven't had time to get a haircut in a while," he hedged.

"Or shave? Or put in your contacts? I had no idea you even wore contacts." She stared at his thick glasses like a spider was perched on top of them. "Can you take them off?"

Winston shook his head. "Not if I want to see, I can't. And I want to stare at your loveliness."

Elizabeth looked around uncomfortably. Winston laughed as he tried to guess the thoughts bouncing around in her head. Were they being watched? Were people feeling sorry for her being seen with this unstylish nerd? She scooted so that her back was to most of the restaurant. Suddenly, she wished she had chosen a less conspicuous restaurant. Well, mostly she wished Winston was his normal, good-looking, devil-may-care self instead of this pin-up boy from the geek academy. People were definitely staring, all right. Wasn't that Jeffrey Goldenray? Oh no. Was he coming over to their table?

"Elizabeth, so good to see you," Jeffrey gushed. "You are looking fabulous as usual. I saw you arrive in that gorgeous limo. You always know how to make an entrance." He shot her date a look and almost burst out laughing. The guy had pop-bottle glasses and an unshaven look that went perfectly with his bedhead. If he was trying to look cool, he had failed miserably. His pinstriped suit may have been from Walmart. And Elizabeth had blushed a garish shade of pink in embarrassment. What a fun little visit this had turned out to be. He hesitated, looking back and forth between Elizabeth and her date, obviously waiting for an introduction.

"Jeffrey, always good to see you as well. In fact, I have a few things to discuss with you. When would be a good time to drop by your office?"

Jeffrey was intrigued. What could Elizabeth want to discuss with him? Maybe she was moving her account to his brokerage. Or it could be any of the other pies he had his hands in. He decided to save his witty, unkind comments for another time. He wouldn't want to lose a delectable new client, he thought hastily.

"I will make any time work for you," Jeffrey said graciously. "Just give my secretary a jingle, and I will meet you at a moment's notice. I look forward to it. Again, you look absolute stunning tonight. It was a pleasure to see you. Ta-ta!"

He whipped around and sauntered off, looking pleased with himself. Winston watched him, amused. "Who was that?" he asked.

"Nobody," Elizabeth said, sounding bored.

"Nobody? Well, what do you need to discuss with him?" Winston asked, totally curious.

"Oh, I don't have anything to discuss with him. I just wanted to be rid of him, and that seemed like the quickest way." She looked at her finger-nails, picked at one, then reached into her purse for a file. She successfully ignored Winston for quite a while. Winston was content to let her think, to sort things out, to find the quickest way to get rid of him too. He studied the gourmet menu with braised quail in blueberry sauce and lemon couscous, crab cakes with goat cheese on a bed of wild rice, and smoked salmon pâté with a specially seasoned tenderloin and bruschetta.

Winston couldn't resist saying, "I think I'm going to order spaghetti. How about you?"

"Spaghetti? Do you mean macaroni and cheese off the kids' menu? Should we just find the closest Burger King?" Elizabeth said sharply.

"Oh, can we? I definitely have a Whopper craving going on." He smiled hugely, enjoying toying with her.

"You are definitely dressed more appropriately for a Burger King than for a brand-new five-star restaurant where the ketchup costs more than an entire Happy Meal," she snapped. "In fact, if you lost a few more pounds, you could pass for Jack Skellington."

He pretended to look offended. "You don't like my new look? I was trying to copy those male models from that *Whole New Man* magazine you've been raving about. I thought I looked just like the dude on page 73.

Elizabeth choked. "You look nothing like Nathan Tucker!" she exclaimed. "Or any of those 'dudes,'" she mocked, "in *Whole New Man* magazine! What is wrong with you? What has happened to you? You've changed. And I don't just mean your look. It's like you're not even the same person anymore." She crossed her arms and pouted.

Even Elizabeth had noticed that he'd changed. He didn't think she noticed much beyond physical appearance. He was also jarred that she knew which model was on page 73 by name. She was smarter and more observant than he thought. Yeah, he was correct in not wanting to cross her, but what did that say that they had dated this long and he didn't know that? Their relationship had been a sham of appearances, and he was just as guilty. But he *had* changed. He just hadn't realized how much until now.

"You're right," he said. He couldn't keep the incredulity out of his voice. "I have changed. I have a different view on life now."

"What happened?" Elizabeth asked.

"I think I grew up," he admitted sheepishly.

Elizabeth laughed. "You grew up?"

But Winston was nodding furiously. "Yeah, finally. Instead of getting all my happiness out of life by going to parties and new restaurants and hanging out with friends at the beach, I'm finding deep satisfaction in discovering my ability to retain information and apply it. I'm enjoying the intricacies of the law and learning new things. I'm finally able to relate to my father in a way that I never have. Probably because I finally grew up. Thanks, Elizabeth, for helping me figure that out," he said genuinely.

"You're welcome," she said, dryly. "But I don't think anyone ever resented your boyish charm. Everyone found it fun and refreshing."

"That's kind of you, Elizabeth. But I'm kind of liking the new me." He looked down at his clothes. "Except for this. I don't think this new look fits me after all. I guess I was looking for a way to express my inner changes."

"Well, that's a relief," Elizabeth said. Then her brow furrowed. "But I don't know how this is going to affect our relationship going forward. I think we may have already drifted too far apart. What is it you want in life?"

"Well," Winston took a deep breath, envisioning his future. "I'm excited I passed the bar. I'm hoping to work in my father and grandfather's firm, but I want to find balance so that I never work the crazy hours he does." Suddenly he realized something he hadn't seen coming. "I think I'm ready to settle down and have a family," he said in wonder.

Elizabeth's eyes grew wide, and she held up her hands. "Whoa, whoa there," she said, sounding panicked. "I'm definitely not."

Winston smiled at her reassuringly. "That's okay," he said. "I'm kind of shocked that came out of my mouth and that I actually feel it's true. I have changed quite a lot. Thanks for helping me to see just how much and figure out what I want in the future. You're pretty amazing, you know."

"Thanks," she answered, sounding more sincere than she had in a long time. "Friends?" she asked.

"Friends," Winston answered, and he ordered the braised quail instead of spaghetti.

Chapter 18 —————————————————

Good News

WINSTON TAPPED LIGHTLY ON his father's office door, then gently pushed it open. His father looked up, smiled, and took off his reading glasses.

"Son, this is a pleasant surprise. What brings you to the office?"

"Well, I actually—"

"Is it Allie? How is she doing? Your mother really likes her, you know. And I know I was a little hard on you at first for what you did. But the more I've thought about it, the more I've realized that took guts. I'm proud of you, Winston."

That rocked Winston a little. He couldn't remember the last time his father told him he was proud of him. It had been so long it had become a distant memory. In fact, it took so much effort to receive recognition from his father that Winston had eventually given up. He was proud of him? And he hadn't even told him that he passed the bar exam. What a day!

"Thanks, Dad. She is doing well. She loves college. She loves Jenna, of course. I think she likes everything about her life. Dad, I think she would be happy living in a cardboard box as long as she was away from her husband."

Jonathan nodded soberly. "You made this new life possible for her, Winston. I'm glad to hear she is well and happy. You should bring her to our house for dinner sometime soon. Your mother would enjoy that. And so would I."

"I could definitely do that. I haven't seen much of Allie lately, and it would be great to have dinner with you as well."

"But, sorry, I interrupted you. Let's start again. Son, this is a pleasant surprise," he said, winking. "What brings you to the office?"

Winston smiled. He couldn't remember the last time he felt this happy in his father's presence. "I have another surprise up my sleeve. Oh, wait. I guess it's in my pocket." He pulled his results out with a flourish. "Sir, may I present my exam results and beg the honor of working with you in this fine establishment."

Jonathan looked like he was going to have a heart attack. No, he looked like he'd been tasered. A deer frozen in the headlights. He examined the results and then Winston. Winston finally realized that his father must have completely given up on the idea of Grover & Grover ever becoming Grover & Grover & Grover. Or maybe Grover & Sons? The name didn't matter, it was just the fact that his father must have completely given up on the dream of him ever becoming a lawyer and joining the firm. Jonathan's look of shock changed to blinking furiously at the tears forming in the corners of his eyes. That look then changed to one of wondrous joy.

He gave a whoop and jumped up, springing toward Winston with arms akimbo, ready for a hug. Winston had known his father would be happy. Pleased seemed more realistic. Possibly exasperated that it had taken his son so ridiculously long. But he had not foreseen this. He laughed and backslapped his father, echoing the joyous celebration.

His father grabbed his arms and looked at him. "I am so happy and proud of you, Winston. You can't possibly know how much." Tears threatened for Winston now.

"I think from your reaction I can somewhat gauge the level of your feelings. And I'm just sorry and ashamed it took me so long," Winston said sheepishly.

"Does your mother know?"

"No, I wanted to tell you first."

More tears formed in Jonathan's eyes. "Maybe we could tell her together. I will call and see if she wants to come down for lunch. You game for that?"

"Of course. Now that I'm free from the toils of studying for this, I have a bit of free time," Winston said, his mood jovial. "While we are waiting, we can pin down a few of the details."

"Already negotiating your salary?" Jonathan asked, chuckling.

Winston laughed. "I guess that's a detail we should talk about, but, honestly, I'm more concerned about time than about money."

"What do you mean?" Jonathan asked.

Winston straightened to his full height and looked Jonathan in the eye. "Dad, I'm planning to take over some of your caseload as well as getting new cases of my own. But I will be honest, here. I never want to work the sort of hours you do, and once you are comfortable with my performance, I want you to cut back or retire and spend more time with Mom."

Jonathan backed up and sat down in his office chair, completely off-balance. Winston had never been so forthright with Jonathan before. This was a side of his usually passive son he had never seen. He was rather proud. He liked it. Jonathan had to stifle the grin threatening to break free.

"I see," Jonathan answered levelly. "And how much are you planning on me cutting back, and how much of a caseload are you planning to handle?" Jonathan asked, clearing his throat and unnecessarily tapping a sheaf of papers into place while again trying to smother a grin.

"How many hours are you currently working a week? Fifty? Eighty? I'm planning to work forty-five. That should more than cut your hours in half."

"Well, then—"

Winston held up a hand. "Dad, if you are about to say you will find some more clients so that we will both be plenty busy, then no. Just no. If you are down to fifty hours and you are stressed about only working five hours a week, here's a solution: I will work the entire fifty, and you take Mom on that trip to Europe like she's always wanted."

Jonathan did smile this time. "It sounds like you've thought of everything. But, no, I wasn't going to suggest we increase our caseload—yet, anyway. What I was going to say is that I have full confidence in your abilities, but I want to help you to transition. I am working close to seventy hours a week, currently. Would you be willing to split that? Thirty-five hours a piece? We could work closely together on my current caseload. When you feel comfortable—which I have a feeling will be very soon—I will consider taking your Mom to Europe while you take over here."

Winston was blindsided. Who knew it would be this easy?

But this would also be a test run. He really did want his parents to take a dream vacation together, but what if he hated practicing law? When his father came back, he would have to break the bad news to him. But then again, maybe it wouldn't be so bad.

Only time would tell.

Chapter 19 ───────────────────────────

Sunday Dinner

ALLIE FELT NERVOUS AS she rode with Winston in his blue Maserati to his parents' house for Sunday dinner. But she was excited for the opportunity to meet Mr. Grover and thank him for his help.

Jonathan was all charming formality and excitement as he came forward to shake Allie's hand. "Thank you for coming to the celebration!" he said exuberantly. "Winston has passed the bar and joined me at the firm, and I could not be happier." He beamed at Winston, and Winston beamed back. "And I think we should also celebrate you for coming into our lives in such a remarkable way."

"I'm so happy for both of you, and I'm so thankful for you and your son and everything you have done for me," Allie said, adopting Jonathan's formal demeanor for only a second before asking, "Could I please give you a hug?"

When he smiled, she wrapped her arms around him and said, "Thank you so much, Mr. Grover. I so appreciate your support and what you have done for me, getting my identification to enroll in school. I have loved it."

Like Grace, Jonathan couldn't remember the last time he had been hugged by someone outside the family. Allie's genuine gratitude and lack of pretense was a refreshing change from the people he encountered on a daily basis. He couldn't help but smile. Grace came up to him and held his hand, her way of expressing that she, too, was grateful for her husband's help and his warm reception of Allie.

"Winston and Grace have told me a lot about your story. I am glad I have been able to be of assistance. In fact, I hope I will be even more helpful in the future with the other matter." Everyone knew exactly what he meant.

"Thank you," Allie said sincerely. "I hope I can one day do something to repay all of you. Your son saved my life that day. All of you have treated me far better than I deserve, with a generosity that takes my breath away. You have a wonderful wife and son."

Jonathan smiled even broader. "Yes, I do," he agreed, feeling the truth and impact of her words. For all of the impatience he had felt toward Winston for so long, he had always recognized what a good man Winston was and what a warm heart he possessed. And Allie had managed to shed light on that. She had worked some magic on him and changed him enough that he'd finally settled down and passed the bar. Jonathan was grateful. "And you have already repaid us," he said warmly.

He looked around at all the happy faces and felt a closeness to his family that had been lacking for a long time. "You have made a positive difference in our lives already. Now, who's ready to eat?"

℘ ℘

"So how did it go at Winston's parents' house?" Jenna asked that night.

Allie loved her chats with Jenna. She couldn't decide if Jenna was more like a big sister, a mother, or trusted friend. She definitely was the wisest, most mature, most experienced of the group. She seemed to genuinely care about each one of her roommates like a big sister would.

If her brother had lived, how would he have treated her? Allie wondered. If he had lived, everything would have been different. Her brother would have taken care of the ranch, and Allie would have been allowed to stay in school. They never would have turned to the Tacklemans for help. She would not have been forced to marry Gary! Her father would not have worked himself into an early grave or spent his last years living in bitterness, anger, and regret. Just as her newfound faith was flickering, she faltered. Why had God let this happen? Why had He taken her brother and ruined the lives of every member of her family?

Jenna was happy for Allie and genuinely liked her, but every time Winston came around and Jenna saw how much he cared about Allie, she was reminded of what she was missing out on. This was so hard! Did Winston know what this was doing to her? If she hadn't blown it, she could be the one spending time with the Grovers.

Jenna sighed. Even though she wished things had worked out for her and Winston, she was happy for Winston and Allie. Truly. He was the kind of guy any girl would proudly take home to her mother. He was rich, handsome, successful, funny, kind, and now a newly polished version of himself. And she realized the amazing transformation was because of Allie. Allie's sweetness had brought out the best in Winston and eliminated his less desirable characteristics. Interesting. She had turned a rough stone into polished rock. The old Winston hadn't been marriage material, but the new Winston was the man of every woman's dreams.

Jenna was the serious one, the nurturer of the group, the one who could be counted on, the one people turned to when they had a problem, and so she was surprised when Allie was so perceptive of her own inner struggles.

Allie had told her about how well the dinner went but stopped abruptly when she saw how sad Jenna was. "What's the matter, Jenna?" Allie asked. "I can tell something is bothering you."

Jenna sighed. She definitely couldn't tell the truth. "Hey, yeah. I'm just super jealous that Winston, who used to like me, now likes you. And worse, you bring home some guy from school, and I'm super attracted to him, too, but he's off-limits. And to top it all off, you're married."

Instead, she said, "I just have a lot of concerns right now. Thank you for noticing, but they are nothing compared to the things you have gone through. I hate to even complain. I sure have enjoyed seeing you so happy. You are happy, aren't you?"

"Oh yes," Allie exclaimed. "I love college, and learning, and freedom, and new friends. I love you, Jenna!" She swooped down to give her friend a hug. "'I'm just so grateful you came into my life. I never really had a friend before I met you." Her eyes grew distant. "Before, I only had one friend."

"Who? Why didn't they help you?"

"He did help me."

"Oh, do you mean Winston?"

"No. Winston is my friend now, but my only friend back in South Dakota was Jesus. I talked to Him all the time. He comforted me. He helped me. He kept me company."

Jenna hugged her tightly. She couldn't answer past the huge lump that formed in her throat just then.

Chapter 20 ───────────────────────────────────

Finals

"I CAN'T BELIEVE THAT was our last literature class," Daniel said. "The semester sure went by fast."

"I agree, but I'm feeling super nervous about the lit final," Allie confessed. "In my other classes, I feel fairly confident that I have learned the material and can answer most of the questions correctly. But literature . . . yikes! It's going to be an interpretative essay. The first thing the professor commented on was that I needed to brush up on my writing skills. I don't grasp the material like you do." She sighed.

"Really, there's nothing to worry about," Daniel said. "Unlike other tests, interpretative essays don't really have right or wrong answers. It's a presentation of your own views and ideas. You'll do fine."

But Allie didn't feel fine.

"Hey," he said, taking her arm. "Really, you'll do great. We've always had good discussions about the books. I've liked what you've said, and the professor will too."

"Thanks," she said, sighing. "Part of it is I think I have some of the books mixed up. I mean, I know what characters are from which book and the plots, but specific scenes—I think maybe I have jumbled them up in my head."

"How about if I come over to your apartment the night before the exam, and we go through the eight books and do a refresher?"

Allie sagged with relief. "Oh, Daniel, would you? That would be so helpful. So Thursday night, then?" Then she had a thought. "How about I make dinner and we eat before we study?"

"I could bring a pizza or something so you won't have to worry about it," he offered.

"No, cooking relaxes me, and it can be a thank-you for helping me study for the exam. I have no doubt you will ace it. In fact, you could probably teach the class just as good as the professor," Allie said.

"Thanks, Allie. That makes me feel like a million bucks. Remember, I've read these books a lot. But I'm impressed with you and how well you've done, reading them for the first time," he said. "See you Thursday."

Allie was in the middle of searing the steaks, browning some mushrooms, and mixing the filling for twice-baked potatoes, so she asked Jenna to please get the door and entertain Daniel for a few minutes. Then they all sat down to dinner together.

"Isn't she a great cook?" Jenna asked Daniel, who nodded. "She's also a great roommate. I've been lucky to get to know her this semester. How about you, Daniel? Do you have good roommates?"

Daniel had them both clutching their sides in fits of laughter as he shared some of the things his roommates did. "One time, Randall left the second-story window open a crack, borrowed a ladder from the apartment complex handyman, filled a bucket with water, climbed up, and dumped the whole bucket on his roommate, who was still sleeping at one in the afternoon."

"You are kidding!" Allie exclaimed. "It's hard for me to believe that some people live these crazy, fun, lighthearted lives. I mean most people." She shook her head. "I am so glad I've been able to experience this."

Jenna gave her a hug. "We are too!"

"Do you want us to dump a bucket of water on you while you're sleeping so you can experience that for yourself?" Daniel asked teasingly. Allie punched him in the arm.

Jenna turned back to Daniel. "What did the guy do?"

"Eric? He woke up sputtering and drenched and yelled something like, 'I'm drowning!'—or maybe it was, 'I'm not thirsty!' Yeah, I think it was, 'I'm not thirsty!'"

"Too funny! And did he get Randall back?"

"Oh yeah, that's also a good story," he said. He glanced over at Allie. They had all finished eating, and Allie had cleared away the dishes. Now she had pulled out her books and was looking through her notes. When had that happened? Daniel wondered. He had been having such a good time he hadn't noticed. Jenna was also startled by how late it was.

"So sorry," she apologized. "I'll get out of your hair and let you study."

Daniel watched as she left the room, hoping he could share the story of Eric's revenge on Randall another time. He rubbed his hands together. "Okay. Study time. Let's do a quick synopsis of each book. Sound good?"

"Absolutely," Allie said. "Should we start with *Divergent*?"

∽ ∾

The exam went well the next day, but it was an entire week before results were posted and their exams were returned. Allie was afraid to look. She had done well on most of her other finals, earning solid Bs. Having dropped out of eighth grade, she was delighted to have done so well. But this was the class she was most worried about.

"Well?" Daniel asked, wanting to see Allie's results.

"I'm afraid to look," Allie said with a self-deprecating, lopsided grin. She handed it to him. "Here, you look, please."

She studied his face as he turned it over and looked at the mark scribbled at the top. His face looked surprised, then joyous.

"Did I get a B?" she asked, hopeful at his reaction.

He shook his head. "Well, that's okay," she said. "I will still be happy with a C. Did I get a C?" she asked.

Daniel turned it over. "You got an A!" he said. "I'm so proud of you." She rushed to hug him, and he whirled her around. "Good job!"

"Thanks, Daniel! I couldn't have done it without you. My treat at the café, today!"

"Oh yeah, we are celebrating, for sure," Daniel said happily.

"Just one thing," Allie said. "Do you mind if I invite Jenna? I think she is at the library this morning and could probably join us."

"Mind? I'd love it," Daniel said.

And Allie felt ecstatic.

—————————————————————————————

Chapter 21

Time with Allie

Now that Winston was done using every spare moment to study for the bar and had finally broken up with Elizabeth, he found it harder and harder to stay away from Allie. She'd astounded him with how well she'd done in her first semester of college, and he was excited to spend more time with her during her break.

He loved that she was thriving. Her excitement was contagious. Just being around her made him feel alive. He loved her inquisitive, problem-solving mind. He loved to bounce ideas off her for his cases. She often had practical insights that he lacked. She was also intuitive. He would go visit her, feeling preoccupied, and she had a way of getting to the root of the problem. She had the uncanny ability to draw it out of him. Just talking out loud made the puzzle seem clearer, the frustration better.

Practicing law became a humbling and eye-opening experience for Winston. He had no idea of the troubles and suffering out there. As he handled more and more workers' compensation cases, he discovered that people who got hurt on the job were often manual laborers. And, as such, many were less-educated and lower-paid. Usually, by the time he took on a case, these people had gone through the correct legal channels in the hopes of getting their medical bills paid—medical bills that were a result of torn rotator cuffs, blown-out knees, back injuries, and the like, on the job.

Winston was appalled by the number of claims denied by the insurance companies, whose doctors argued that the injuries were because of age or preexisting conditions. Even in clear-cut cases of negligence, they low-balled the workers who lacked knowledge of the system and what they were entitled to.

Winston started telling Allie about his current case, sure that her eyes would glaze over. Instead, she surprised him.

"Can I help research the case, Winston? I love looking up stuff on the internet," Allie begged. "Plus, I'm going to need something to do with my time during the break. You know how stir-crazy I get."

Winston nodded. "True, true. Sure, why not?" he answered.

Later, Winston laughed when she showed him what she found. A few clicks and she smiled up at him. He leaned forward to look at the monitor. The information would be super helpful to his case. "Good work, Allie. I'll put you on the payroll."

She laughed. "I already am, but now I'm doing something to earn it," she quipped. "So what's my next assignment?"

He grinned. He could already think of three different cases he could use her research skills on.

"Could I hire you permanently?" Winston asked.

Allie chuckled.

"No, I'm serious," Winston said. "You are so good with the clients and a wiz at the research. I couldn't find a better assistant if I accepted résumés from across the country. Plus," he looked at her steadily, "I enjoy working with you."

She smiled. "I love the work. I couldn't think of anything I'd enjoy more. Except I do love learning. Can I work for you part-time and still work on my degree?"

"Of course," Winston said. "And while I am serious that I do want you to work for me forever, I don't want you to do it if you don't want to. I think it completely needs to be your choice. You've had too many decisions taken away from you over the years."

Besides help with research, Winston needed Allie's help and advice for other situations—including when he won his first case, which involved a man who had been assigned to help back up a large rig that did not have backup cameras. The man had slipped on a patch of ice as the truck was maneuvering. The driver didn't see him, thought the coast was clear, and backed up over him, crushing a few fingers.

The compensation he was offered was embarrassingly low. They went back and forth among the other lawyers, trying to settle the matter out of court. About the time Winston was going to give up and take the case to trial, they came through with a good offer. The client invited Winston to coffee to celebrate.

Winston asked what he planned to do with the money and what he planned to do for a living in the future because he wouldn't want to keep working at the warehouse anymore.

The man surprised him by saying he didn't plan to switch jobs. All his buddies worked at the warehouse, and he'd probably use whatever money he had left after paying his medical bills to treat his friends to rounds of beer for as long as the money held out.

Winston had stewed and worried about the guy for days. What if he got hurt again? What would he do if he weren't healthy enough for manual labor? He couldn't sleep at night for worrying about the guy.

Finally, he asked Allie what she thought. She prayed for the man and suggested Winston do the same. He asked for inspiration on anything he might do to impact the man's future for the good. They both reached the same answer. Winston needed to somehow steer him to a new career path.

He took the guy out to lunch and asked him about what things interested him. He also brought a brochure and list of classes from the local trade school. The guy again surprised him. He was interested in both welding and computers and agreed to enroll in classes at the trade school. Winston went with him to get him signed up and made sure it was all set up in advance and that his rent was paid in advance so he could get through the next few months of schooling.

Winston would not have had such success without Allie.

Now he was working on a case where a school janitor had twisted his knee on some gravel as he was taking a heavy load of kitchen garbage out to the dumpster. Ignoring it for a while, he'd put too much strain on his good knee. Now both were in bad shape. Each day at work was agony.

Winston could not believe the compassion he felt for his clients. It gave him a whole new appreciation for the privileges and ease he had grown accustomed to throughout his life. And it felt so good to fight on their behalf and try to make a difference in their lives and help them get the compensation that was rightfully theirs.

More than anything, he enjoyed sharing the cases with Allie and having her work beside him. She grew increasingly adept at finding the right information. She became a key part of his practice, and she was so good with the clients. She had so much compassion and empathy. In many ways, she knew how they felt. Winston was relying on her more and more and was amazed at her people skills and uncanny insights.

When he compared Allie to Elizabeth and the other women he'd dated, he was shocked at the difference and appalled that he'd ever found those women attractive. Sure, they were appealing on the outside.

He shuddered to think he had been seriously contemplating proposing to Elizabeth. What would his life have been like if he had married her? Shallowly making appearances at all the social events and focusing on the things she found important, like fame, fortune, and status. It could very possibly have been cold and loveless in the end. At this point, it was hard to imagine.

Chapter 22 ――――――――――――――――――――――――――――

Christmas

ALLIE HAD NEVER EXPERIENCED such a Christmas.

The contrast between last Christmas and this Christmas was enough to make her laugh—or cry. Last year, Gary had expected her to cook a full turkey dinner with mashed potatoes, gravy, stuffing, rolls, and pie. For a gift, he'd given her a new saddle. She liked the new saddle, but instead of being a surprise, it was an absolute necessity. Her old saddle was beyond repair and should have been replaced years before. Gary had also purchased a new TV for both of them. But Allie never had time to watch TV, and Gary knew it. In fact, he'd sat there most of Christmas Day enjoying it while she slaved away in the kitchen. She didn't mind cooking, but she was exhausted and would much rather have spent her "day off" resting. After hours of work, the meal was consumed in less than half an hour. She asked Gary if he would help with the cleanup, but he just laughed and went back to the TV and took a nap. Allie had wanted to cry.

But then something miraculous had salvaged the day and made it memorable. It also cemented a pattern of hope for the next year as she prayed for escape. Instead of crying over the dishes, she said a prayer, asking God for strength and comfort. She'd prayed she could remember the miraculous gift God had given to all—that of His Son, Jesus Christ, and the atoning sacrifice and Resurrection that would redeem all people. She'd pictured the new baby wrapped in swaddling clothes and lying in a manger in a humble stable, with a loving mother and father watching over

Him, a bright new star spotlighting Him from the heavens, and shepherds and wise men journeying by foot or camel to worship the newborn King. Suddenly the dishes were done, the dreaded task completed before she'd even finished her prayer, and instead of feeling physically drained, she felt energized and lighthearted.

This Christmas she prayed in gratitude. She was just as grateful for the Christ Child, but she had so much more to be grateful for.

This Christmas, she spent the morning with her roommates, exchanging gifts and singing Christmas carols off-tune at the top of their lungs. She sat under the tree, which she had helped decorate, basking in its colorful, glowing lights. They had hot chocolate and crepes with strawberries and cream.

That afternoon, Winston whisked her off to his parents' house for a delicious dinner. She didn't cook a single thing for it. She offered to help clean up, and they laughed. She was turned down flat.

The atmosphere at the Grover's was happy and festive. The formal stiffness Jenna always talked about had been replaced with a comfortable closeness. Allie basked in the feeling of warmth. She felt completely welcome and a part of things. She loved Amanda's two children. They made the holiday so special, excited over every tiny surprise.

After dinner, the family moved from the dining room into the kitchen.

"We are starting a new tradition this year," Grace announced proudly. "A gingerbread contest!" She gestured to the kitchen's enormous island, which had sheets of gingerbread, vast bowls of frosting, and cheery bowls of Skittles, red hots, Smarties, gumdrops, bubble gum, gummy bears, and other candies.

"Can we eat some of it, Grandma?" Lydia asked, wide-eyed and already dragging a barstool over to where most of the candies were.

Grace laughed. "Of course you can. There's plenty. But let's not overdo it, or you will end up with a tummy ache. How about one of everything?"

"Yeah!" Lydia was already reaching into the bowl.

Instead of just imagining the Christmas story unfolding, Allie listened to it read from the Bible by Winston's father. The sweet little grandchildren posed at Mary and Joseph, complete with stuffed-animal props and costumes made of robes and towels. Allie clapped when it was over, complimenting Amanda on what darling, well-behaved children she had. Amanda beamed. She had been shocked and dismayed when she'd first heard Allie's story but had taken to her as quickly and protectively as the rest of the family.

So this year, in contrast to last, Allie felt loved. Even though her roommates and every member of the Grover family had given her a wonderful pile of fun and presents, their love was the best gift she had ever been given.

Chapter 23

Depressed

IT WAS FRIDAY NIGHT, and Winston was depressed. Some of the cases were really hard. His head was spinning with the latest regarding a poor farm laborer who had lost three fingers while trying to fix a large produce conveyor belt. Winston was tired of working and worrying.

He called Allie to see what she was doing that night. He could really use her insight and research skills. And, if he was being honest with himself, he needed her companionship. But she was studying with that guy Daniel again. Did she like him? For some reason, that really bothered Winston. At least it really bothered him tonight. He felt edgy, but he couldn't pinpoint why.

The phone rang. Tessa. Winston answered with a smile, quickly agreeing to go out clubbing that night. From his massive closet, he pulled a shirt he hadn't worn in ages. He felt his heartbeat quicken with anticipation. It had also been a long time since he had gone out for some fun with Tessa and the girls. He raced off in the Porsche, was quickly escorted to the VIP line, and then ushered by the bouncers into the heart of the club. Tessa greeted him with a kiss and immediately whisked him off to the dance floor.

But it wasn't long before he realized he was *not* having a good time.

"What am I doing?" he said out loud, although his voice was inaudible over the ear-splitting, pulsating music.

The spotlights bouncing off the disco ball into brilliant fragments of flashing light had lost their appeal. Instead of dazzling and mesmerizing him and creating excitement, they gave him a headache and put him in a bad mood. Had he all of a sudden grown old or something? He couldn't figure it out.

"Cheers!" Tessa clinked glasses with him and downed her champagne, not even savoring the expensive drink.

Winston felt miserable and downed a whiskey. Then another. Then another. How could Tessa and the girls do this week after week, night after night? he wondered.

"What's the matter?" Tessa yelled. And Winston could still hardly hear her. Tessa's eyes followed her friends as they jumped, moved, and grooved to the beat.

"Let's go dance," Tessa invited, pulling Winston along with her. As they made their way through the dancing, bouncing, gyrating crowd, women smiled at him, winked at him, flirted with him, asked him to dance. But it wasn't fun anymore. It used to be his favorite thing. Now he just wanted to go home, maybe give Allie a call if it wasn't too late, and see how her day had gone. But what if she was still out with Daniel? He felt himself sinking deeper into a depression. Part of him wanted to stay here and get plastered.

As he threw back another drink and watched the dance-floor mob bouncing to the beat, he remembered that next week was a special governor's gala and he had not yet invited Allie to go with him. He remembered her talking about all the things she wanted to do and how she had never had the opportunity to attend a school dance. This wasn't a school dance, but it was a huge step up. He knew she would love it. He mentally planned many of the details of the date. He would get a limo again and take Allie for a five-star dining experience. He started getting excited thinking about the weekend ahead and Allie's reaction to it. Just thinking about a date with Allie had his mood soaring.

Now, it was time to get out of here. He looked around the club, soaking in the details, knowing it would be his last time.

He considered driving himself home. The old Winston would have. Instead, he called Sebastian, instructing him to take a taxi so he could drive a slightly-drunk Winston home in the Porsche.

Yeah, his life had changed, all right.

Now, how should he ask his date to the dance? he mused happily while he waited.

Chapter 24 ——————————————————————

The Gala

ALLIE HAD NEVER FELT more beautiful. And it was hard to beat the first time she'd stepped out of an expensive salon in designer clothes that transformed her from frumpy cowgirl to Hollywood chic—she, who hadn't ever had her hair professionally cut and had previously worn only thrift-store or church-donated castoffs. But now she had combined her new looks with fairy-tale dance queen.

Last week, Winston had asked her if she'd like to attend the governor's Business Innovators and Success Committee's Annual Gala—as his date. "It's the closest us grown-ups get to attending a school dance," he'd said.

"A dance? Could I wear a sparkly ball gown? Like a formal?"

She'd picked a sophisticated, pale-pink, body-hugging designer dress and felt like she had stepped out of a fashion magazine. And from the way Winston's eyes had practically popped out of his head, he must have thought so too. She couldn't wait to walk into the gala on his arm.

She gave a twirl.

"Pose for photos," he instructed Allie, laughing. And Sailor, Katie, and Jenna all pulled out their cell phones, commanding them to say cheese. Winston presented her a bouquet of pink roses to enjoy later, as well as a wrist corsage of pink roses with lace, satin, and baby's breath.

"Now, don't stay out too late," Jenna said, playfully scolding them. She, Katie, and Sailor had made the moment memorable for a girl who had never been able to experience a prom or dance.

⤳ ⤳

"Your limo awaits," Winston said, bowing gallantly, then offering his elbow to escort this beauty to the limo. He couldn't help contrast this evening with the last time he had ordered a limo. He hadn't even bothered to get out of the car that night. Well, he couldn't, or it would have ruined his plans for the breakup. That night he had dreaded. This night, he had worked hard to make everything special.

"Oh, Winston! A limousine. You are too good to me. Thank you. I will never forget this evening, ever. You are absolutely the best," Allie said as she tugged on his elbow. When he bent over, she kissed his cheek. The gesture was somehow devastating. Winston had to work to compose himself. This dear woman. Her innocence, sweetness, and courage had taught him so much. He would do anything for her.

He took her to an upscale restaurant with simple yet elegant food. Large lanterns were interspersed with chandeliers, giving an eclectic but elegant and romantic atmosphere. A single scented candle burned on their table, its flickering light making Allie's face look even more enchanting.

⤳ ⤳

Allie's heart thudded as she looked at Winston. She should not be looking at a man like this. She was married! She shouldn't be looking for a Prince Charming when she was bound to somebody else. Part of her wanted to say that indulging in this fantasy wasn't hurting anyone, but the more she gave her heart to Winston, the deeper her pain would be when she had to give him up once and for all. She knew that Gary would never divorce her. She would never be free. And Winston would never be hers. It was a sobering thought. She had to be content with being friends. And eventually, when he married, she would somehow have to find a way to be fine with that too.

Arriving at the courthouse, she felt like a film star when the limo opened and she was escorted down the red carpet.

The inside of the courthouse was also alive with light, flowers, candelabras, and elegant little tables and chairs arranged off the dance floor near a lectern.

Winston whisked her away to dance, and Allie felt she was floating in his arms. Several people came up to be introduced, obviously wanting to ask her to dance. Just like a high schooler would jealously guard his date, Winston guarded her that evening. Allie was so glad. For all the people skills she had gained over the last few months, Allie had no desire to dance with any among the array of potential dance partners, young or old, rotund or beanpole. She loved dancing, especially the slow songs, when she felt Winston's warm hand on her back and she could just enjoy the quiet strength of his presence and the music as they swayed. She wanted the night to end with a kiss but berated herself with the ongoing chant that she was a married woman.

The festivities were briefly interrupted by refreshments. While they enjoyed their crème brûlée and cheesecake, the mayor gave a brief spiel about the apartments they had recently completed for low-income families. Allie clapped politely as a few contractors and government officials received awards. She had enjoyed helping Winston with the legalities of the project. Then Winston's name was called to receive an award.

"Come with me," he said, holding out his hand. "I could not have done it without you."

Allie could not resist the proffered hand. She stood at Winston's side as he accepted the award and then handed it to her. "This is my valuable assistant," he said, purposely leaving out her name. "We have felt honored to work on this project and for the difference it can make in so many lives. We respect their hard work to take care of themselves and their families and to overcome difficult circumstances. They are well-deserving, and I know they will live happy and productive lives in their new homes, which will bless many generations to come. They have my full respect and support."

The clapping was loud and spontaneous. The desserts were cleared, and they went back to dancing. Each time she floated across the dance floor, she fell harder and harder for Winston, but she kept telling herself it was wrong and to think of Gary instead.

If only she had been able to follow through with those good intentions.

Still, her one and only high school substitute dance would be a night to cherish all her life. And it did not even end with a kiss.

Shocked

"And finally, tonight, for our feel-good segment of the news, dignitaries in L.A. came together for a special gala to honor those who sacrificed their time, materials, or labor to build these new apartments for the impoverished of the inner city. Check out the before and after shots."

Clips showed the governor at the ribbon cutting in the neighborhood where the improvements had taken place, shots of some of the happy tenants moving into their new homes, the construction workers who had labored for months on the improvements, and then finally a colorful array of photos of people at the gala, accepting awards or giving speeches at the pulpit.

Gary gaped at the TV. A solid-gold bat to the head couldn't have hit him harder.

For there, in the background, looking like the moon was hung by the guy next to her, was Alexandria.

Alexandria! He had thought she was dead. After the initial disbelief, he felt a jolt of anger. Alexandria!

He had stayed in California for another two weeks after the official search ended. Instead of restlessly walking up and down the same stretch of beach, he had taken a more practical approach to his search.

If Alexandria had used that opportunity when Gary was hit by the volleyball to disappear but she didn't have any friends or money, he had to figure out what she would have done next. Without money or ID, she would have had to find a job and a place to stay. He'd started searching the restaurants and hotels close to the beach. He still had his wife's picture with him.

"Have you seen this woman? Does she work here?" he'd asked again and again.

And time and again, the clerks, cooks, and shop owners shook their heads. Gary had widened his search. Nothing. But he was always watching, half expecting to see his wife's face at any moment—waitressing tables, wearing a maid uniform, taking out trash, even hunkering under bridges or in shelters among the hordes of homeless. After another two weeks of hunting, he'd finally given up. If she was alive, she had managed to find a life farther from that beach than he expected.

At the beginning and after what he'd just gone through, going home seemed more like a vacation. But it was empty and lonely. Without Alexandria, the house was too quiet. Meals weren't cooked, toilets weren't scrubbed, floors weren't vacuumed, and fences weren't fixed. Had Alexandria really done all that herself? Gary was in a constant state of exhaustion. Each night, with only the essential chores completed, he stared at the TV like a zombie, trying to rest body and mind for the next grueling day of work. Oh, how he missed his wife!

And, then, there she was! On national television of all things and looking like a beauty-pageant contestant. She had on a long satin ball gown in a becoming shade of pink, with a sexy slit all the way up her thigh.

He thirsted for revenge. But not on Alexandria. He wanted her back. He would get his life back and his wife back. Should he call the police? No, that was the worst possible idea. Alexandria would not want to come here as long as she was with that rich hotshot and going to glamorous events and who knows what else she was up to.

Hmmm. If the guy was rich, Alexandria would have no need to claim the ranch and it would be all his. But then again, if the guy was rich, maybe Gary could get a bigger piece of the cash, maybe even enough to buy back his so-called parents' ranch. Even enough to hire some hands so that he wouldn't have to work like a slave.

But although that sounded appealing, he felt like what he really wanted was to have Alexandria back. She owed him. She was his wife. And no one walked out on him. His wounded pride turned into a blinding rage. He took the fireplace poker and banged it against the rock of the fireplace until a few splinters broke off. Then he turned the poker on the already ragged couch and beat it until some stuffing popped out. He imagined the couch was Allie's boyfriend, and his mouth turned up cruelly.

He needed a plan.

But first he needed to piece together what had happened. He thought back carefully on the moment Alexandria had disappeared. That stupid jerk had knocked him down with a volleyball and then his wife was gone. He had been right all along! That stunt was no accident. That jerk had knocked him down on purpose so that Alexandria could get away. But how did she know anyone in California who would plan this elaborate hoax? It stumped him. He had to find out who the guy on TV was. Then he had to find out how to destroy him.

Chapter 26

An Unwelcome Discovery

ALLIE AND DANIEL HAD developed the habit of going to the student café after their literature class. This semester, they signed up for a course on classics offered by the same professor. Allie looked forward to discussing the books with Daniel, who was insightful and seemed to have read every book imaginable. She needed as much help as she could get. Her writing skills had come a long way, but they were still in need of improvement. She cringed when she remembered the first comment by the professor: "You may need to refresh your writing skills." Refresh! That was a kind way of putting it. She had never developed any writing skills. Fortunately, she took Daniel into her confidence right away, confessing that she was an eighth-grade dropout, and he'd taught her the basics and then proofread most of her papers.

"Did you watch that game the other night?" Jordan, from one of Daniel's other classes, stopped by their table.

"I caught a little of it," Daniel said. "How about you? Do you still have season tickets?"

Jordan smiled broadly. "I do. Pretty sweet seats too. Did you catch the last-second-buzzer three-pointer for the win?"

"I sure did." Daniel high-fived Jordan. "Very awesome!"

"Totally. Well, see you." He waved at Allie and was gone.

Daniel rolled his eyes. "Am I the only one on campus whose father is not a millionaire? What I wouldn't give for great seats at the Lakers' games!"

"Well, my father isn't rich, but I am here because of a friend whose father is rich. I suppose that is just as bad." Allie ducked her head and grimaced.

"Oh, that's right. I saw you. You and Winston Grover," Daniel said, smiling broadly. "You looked amazing in that ball gown."

"You were at the fundraiser gala? Why didn't you say hello? Or ask me to dance?"

Daniel chuckled. "Because I wasn't there."

Who would have taken a picture of her with Winston and shown it to Daniel? she wondered. Plenty of cameras were clicking at the gala, but which photographer knew Daniel? Daniel had met Winston once or twice, but it wasn't as if they were chummy enough to swap photos. "Hey, look at me with your friend Allie" just wasn't Winston's style.

"So how did you see my picture?" she asked.

"I saw you on TV," Daniel said, biting into a ginormous blueberry muffin.

Allie blanched. "TV?" she asked hoarsely. "You saw me on TV? Like a local news broadcast?" She closed her eyes. If it was just local TV, maybe Gary hadn't seen it. And even if he had seen it, maybe he hadn't recognized her with her blonde hair. He hadn't seen her for a long time. And she did look quite a bit different now. She started to breathe again. Maybe it was going to be ok, after all.

Daniel looked surprised. "Are you ok? What's going on?"

"Daniel, we've been friends for a long time. I've been thinking I've needed to tell you the truth for quite a while now."

"What? You're an alien?" he asked, eyes wide with disbelief.

If the moment hadn't been so earth-shatteringly awful, Allie would have burst out laughing.

"What is it?" he asked, looking a bit alarmed. "What's wrong? You suddenly tensed up."

"It's a long story," Allie said, sighing. "I told you I came from South Dakota, right?"

"Yeah?"

Allie didn't spare any details. She found it tumbling out of her. Daniel went from slack-jawed to mouth agape in a few blinks, his expression a mixture of shocked, compassionate, incredulous, and caring.

"Is that why I see you looking over your shoulder so often?" he asked.

"Do I?" She hadn't even realized it.

Daniel nodded. "All the time. I thought you had a stalker ex-boyfriend. Hmmm. I guess I was mostly right." He patted her shoulder. "So, to make sure I've got this straight . . . that's how you became friends with Winston? He rescued you? And then he set you up here at college. And your husband thinks you drowned? He sounds like the stuff nightmares are made of—a real sociopath."

"Are you mad at me for not telling you sooner? I am so sorry. I wanted to so many times. It just never seemed like the right time to say, "Hey, if you have any romantic notions about me, they better stop right now because I'm already married." Allie looked down, then back up at him.

Daniel leaned forward and put his hands on the table, looking Allie in the eye. "I admit that I did have some romantic notions at first. But that first time I went to the apartment and Winston was there, I could sense there was something between you two." He held up a hand when Allie started to interrupt. "Let me finish. And don't worry, I understand a lot better what exactly it is between you and Winston. But I also have to say, I have met someone I am really interested in since then." He looked at her intently, as if she might know who he was referring to. "But I really enjoy our friendship, and I didn't see any reason why we shouldn't hang out anymore. Ok, now that we have our personal feelings out in the open, are you afraid your husband saw you on TV?"

"Terrified. But it was just a local news snippet, right?"

"Local? I think so," Daniel said, nodding. "But didn't you say your in-laws are local?"

"Yeah, they only live about thirty minutes away, I think," she said.

"We are looking at a lot of what-ifs. Chances are good Gary will not have seen the segment and neither have his parents. But I would not stop looking over your shoulder. And when you are on campus, I want to be beside you. I think you should always be with either your roommates or another friend and always take extreme precautions."

"And you just saw it on TV last night? If he did see, how long do you think it would take for him to track me down and get here?" Allie asked.

"How computer savvy is he?" Daniel asked.

"Not very," Allie said, her voice faltering.

"I think you have a few days at least," he said. "I am so sorry, Allie. Thank you for confiding in me."

"I'm just sorry it took me so long," she said.

Back

Unfortunately, Gary's computer skills had improved.

He googled the image of Alexandria at the gala and zoomed in. He had not imagined it. She was looking at the man on her right with obvious adoration. Gary seethed. Who was he? Gary carefully studied the man's features. He found a guest list of bigwigs at the gala. After more searching and googling and clicking, he determined that the man his *wife* seemed besotted with was Winston Jameson Grover, some big-shot lawyer with a main office in downtown L.A. Correction—his father, Jonathan Winston Grover, was the big shot lawyer, but Winston also worked at the firm, he discovered.

He jotted down the address and then zoomed in to find it on the map. Then he checked it for distance against the beach where Alexandria was last spotted. Had she looked up lawyers at home in South Dakota and then bee-lined it to one the second she got away from him? It didn't seem likely. But if that was the case, how did she go from being a potential client to a date at a gala event? What was the connection? How had she found this Grover guy? Were they a couple? The thought infuriated him. He wasn't sure how, but he had to get to California and find his wife and bring her back.

"Back already, Gary?" his mother asked as he barged through the front door of his parents' home in California. "What's going on? Did you hear from the police?"

His dad stared disapprovingly.

The parents were becoming annoying. Already harboring intense anger for having first been hoisted from the ranch he grew up on, to then being foisted onto Alexandria's family, Gary was on a short fuse. Every irritation set him off. And he'd dealt with plenty of irritations since the beginning of this ordeal. "Gary, where are you going? Gary, when are you going to take care of your pile of laundry? Gary, when are you going to give Alexandria up for dead and go back and work on the ranch? And worst of all, "Gary, when are you going to get out and start dating again? You're not getting any younger, and neither are we. We want to see our grandchildren before we leave this mortal life."

Gary wanted to tell them that today *was* the last day of their mortal life because he had had it with them and was going to end the misery for all of them. But he always managed to keep his temper in check. It was hard not having Alexandria around to take his frustrations out on. But he was finding other methods of doing that lately.

He didn't understand their obsession with grandchildren, their endless demands, or why they treated him like dirt. And now he was worried they had sold him out. If they had, they were maybe going to have a little accident, he thought menacingly.

"Yes. She's been sighted," he said evenly, not saying he was the one who had sighted her, and not the police. "But they don't know where she is. She's alive but has amnesia," he lied.

"That's wonderful news!" Martha exclaimed. "Not about the amnesia, of course, but I thought she had died for sure. So it's wonderful that she is still alive. What can we do to help, Gary?"

"Just let me handle it," he said. "But is it okay that I stay here with you while we try to find her?"

"Of course," Martha said, a bit of a twinkle back in her eye—probably a result of the renewed hope of having grandchildren, Gary thought bitterly.

Gary unpacked his suitcase in the tiny guest room. He may as well settle in, he thought. But, optimistically, he hoped the search wouldn't take long. He imagined finding Alexandria and discovering that she indeed had amnesia. Her memory would come flooding back when she saw him, and she would jump into his arms, so happy to see her husband again.

She wouldn't be able to wait to get back to their life, the ranch, and the hard work in South Dakota. Then maybe he could take it easy again, he thought. And maybe they could start their family and bring those coveted grandchildren into his parents' life. The fantasy continued with his parents dying and leaving him a bundle of money—enough to expand the ranch beyond the size it had been when they'd first sold it—and Gary becoming an important rancher with a family. It was a good fantasy, and now it was time to make it happen.

He had the address of the law firm for Grover & Grover and memorized the route. Now he sat out front. Should he wait and watch the people coming out? Or should he go in demanding answers? In all of his planning at home, he had thought through the outcomes of both scenarios. In the first, he would discover what was going on from a distance. Then he could get revenge if he learned he had been double-crossed. The plan required a lot of diligence and patience but could turn out very satisfactorily in the end.

In the second scenario, he could have answers and even his wife back in just a matter of minutes, and that was a very inviting prospect. However, that also brought lots of risk. What if they were her lawyers and were trying to help her push for a divorce? Gary did not want a divorce. Where would he ever find a woman like Alexandria? She was the hardest working, most capable woman he knew of. She could outwork a man. She outworked him for sure. Plus, she was beautiful, smart, caring, and everything he had ever hoped for in a wife. That was why he'd had to guard her so jealously. He couldn't risk her running off or finding or falling for someone else. She belonged to him. He loved her and he knew he would never find another woman her equal. She was unmatched. He could not risk losing her to divorce.

"I guess it's plan A, then," he said to himself. He looked at the clock on the dashboard. It was 4:56. They should be getting off work soon. Then he could follow Winston home. Maybe he would even see Alexandria today, he thought with a surge of hope. By 5:53, Gary was beginning to think he had missed the guy. Maybe he had access to the parking garage across the street by some underground walkway. If so, he could be long gone.

But then the heavy glass door opened and out stepped a man with dark, wavy hair and an expensive tailored suit. The man adjusted dark sunglasses as he entered the glaring sunset, but even so, Gary recognized him from his internet searches. It was Winston Jaymeson Grover, all right.

Gary pulled the black baseball cap low over his brow and exited the car. He discreetly followed Winston at a distance. At this hour in this busy downtown professional district, so many people were coming and going it was easy to follow Winston unnoticed. He entered the parking garage, squinting in the gloom until his eyes readjusted. Winston was striding to his car, his polished dress shoes clicking on the cement. Gary stayed in the shadows and watched Winston pull out his key fob and unlock his Porsche. He looped the leather shoulder bag over his head and tossed it into the passenger seat, then slid behind the wheel. He was peeling out of the garage in record time, and Gary had to hustle to his own waiting vehicle.

In disgust, Gary ripped a neon-orange parking ticket off his windshield. Sheesh, he'd only been gone a minute and a half. He jumped into the car and sped away, hoping the Porsche was stopped at a red light so he could catch it. He circled around, hoping to catch a glimpse, but no luck. Now what? He slammed his fist against the steering wheel. Finally, he drove back to his parents' house.

Like Groundhog Day, Gary tried again the following evening. This time, when he saw Winston emerge from the gleaming building, he was poised and pointed in the direction he saw the Porsche disappear. Throughout the frustrating stop-and-go journey on impossibly clogged streets, Gary swerved and cut, trying to keep up with the blasted Porsche. Finally, the traffic thinned as Gary funneled out of the city and inland toward the posh suburbs. After what seemed like the longest commute ever, making Gary even more grateful to live on a ranch than in the city, he watched Winston turn into a neighborhood, then into a driveway, then into a garage. Gary's eyes about popped out of his head as he took in the grandeur of the mini mansion. If this was where Alexandria had been living, in the lap of luxury no less, how would he manage to convince her to give this up to work like a slave on the ranch? The enormity of the task had Gary questioning for a minute, but it all came down to one thing: she was his wife.

Chapter 28 —————————————————————————

Stalking

"THAT SUSPICIOUS CAR IS back," Winston told Sebastian with concern.

"That old Ford at the end of the street? It's been there most of the day. Do you think I should call the police?"

"What for?"

"It worries me, sir. It could be a mentally unstable client. Pardon me, but it could be a crazy ex-girlfriend or perhaps a wannabe girlfriend stalker. I don't know. I just think it might be a nice precaution."

"What if I just walked up to the car to see who was in it?"

Sebastian shook his head. "Maybe I should be the one to walk up to the car to see who's in it."

This time Winston shook his head. "No way. If the person is some whacko as you suggest, then neither one of us is risking our life just to satisfy our curiosity."

"It could be nothing," Sebastian said.

"Maybe we should put it to the test. Do you think the car would follow me if I left?" Winston asked.

"It would be interesting to find out."

"I want to go to Allie's, but if it is some nut job, of all places, I don't want him to follow me there," Winston said. "In fact, the nut job could be Allie's ex-husband."

"But why would he be staking you out if he's looking for Allie?" Sebastian asked.

"I don't know. But if he did see us on TV like she's afraid of, then what he wants is for me to lead him to Allie," Winston said.

"I could be your decoy," Sebastian offered. "I will take your car. I need to go to the dry cleaners and to the vacuum repair place. You could watch the car, see if it follows me, then leave."

"And if he quits following and doubles back, will you call and let me know?"

"Of course," Sebastian answered.

Sebastian, never one to do things halfway, put on one of Winston's long trench coats, a hat, and some sunglasses before grabbing the keys to the SUV, the vehicle Winston most often drove for errands. The windows weren't as tinted as the Maserati's, but Sebastian hoped his disguise would fool anyone who might be after Winston. He pulled out, going a speed he didn't think would arouse suspicion if someone was lurking in the gray Ford down the road. From behind the sunglasses, Sebastian scouted the interior of the Ford. Someone was definitely there. Hunkered down but definitely there. Sebastian could feel his heart rate accelerate faster than Winston's racecar. Almost turning off the street, he glanced back. The Ford was moving out after him.

"Now's your chance, Winston," Sebastian muttered as the house disappeared in the rearview mirror.

Next time that Ford showed up, Sebastian would have no qualms about calling the police. Or should he call them now? Being followed made his palms sweat. But the dry cleaners was in a bustling neighborhood, where Sebastian felt safe and could get help. But then again, maybe he shouldn't go to the dry cleaners. If he did and the occupant of the car was someone stalking Winston, as soon as they spotted Sebastian, they would realize they had been found out. Winston and Sebastian would no longer have the upper hand. So that meant he also couldn't call the police or purposely shake the car loose. Where to go, and what to do?

He called Winston. "Winston? Did you leave? The gray car is still following me. I can't decide what to do. I think if I get out of the car and he realizes it isn't you, he will feel like you duped him. Then we take away the upper hand."

"Plus, he or she might be violent. It's hard to say with stalkers or psycho ex-husbands."

"It could just be a super pretty woman hoping to catch a glimpse of you."

"Ha-ha," Winston deadpanned without humor. "I'm not that lucky. Or if it is a beautiful woman, she probably has a hatchet."

Sebastian quirked an eyebrow. "Tick off some of the wrong people lately?"

"Just Elizabeth," he answered, releasing a breath of air and sounding pained.

"I thought you left on good terms. Huh. Back to reality. What should I do?" Sebastian asked. "I'm kind of panicking here."

Winston could hear it in his voice. "All right, so you want to have a destination but not let him see you. But I need a little time to get to Allie's, and my flashy car is easy to spot. I know. How about you go through a fast-food drive-thru?"

"Great idea. I can do that."

"Hey! What if you tell the person working the window that you need a description of the person driving the gray Ford. You will pretend someone forgot something in your order, and when you go back through the line, you will have a description of the person following you."

"Good plan, Sherlock. I will report back," Sebastian said.

After ordering, he was invited to drive to the first window to pay his $13.79. The boy taking the order had a dull, glazed-over look that matched his dull voice. Sebastian decided to try his luck with whoever was at the next window instead. He paid the tab and moved on.

The window was already open, a large cup poised at the opening, ready to hand to him. The young woman holding the cup was smiling and had sparkling, intelligent eyes. Sebastian was happy he had waited to talk to her.

"Here's your large Coke. We'll have the rest ready in a minute," she said, handing it through.

"Thanks! Could I ask a favor?"

The woman nodded, likely expecting him to ask for extra hot sauce, not a description of the driver two cars back. But what could it hurt? She took out two of his tacos so he had a legitimate reason to come back through the line.

Sebastian pulled over and made a big show out of going through his sacks and throwing up his arms, indicating that some of his order was missing. He circled around to the back of the line. The gray Ford pulled up to the second window, neck craning to see where Sebastian went.

Sebastian pulled around, explained at the kiosk, and was quickly back at the second., asking for a description of the driver as she handed him his bag of tacos.

Her brows furrowed in concentration. "A man in his early thirties, I think. Weathered skin. Not very attractive. Dark hair and brown eyes, I think."

Sebastian was floored. He would have bet $1,000 the driver was a woman. He didn't want Winston to be right that it could be Allie's abusive husband. But maybe it wasn't. It was a mystery. "What was he like? Mean? Friendly?"

The woman shook her head. "Quiet. He didn't say anything. Not even thank you, like most people do. He did seem preoccupied though."

"Probably because he was worried about me getting away. A man? Hmmm. I didn't see that coming." Not even with all the talk about Allie's husband hunting her down. He handed her a $50 bill. "For you, with many thanks. Have a great evening."

Her face lit up as she took the tip and pocketed it. She waved, then reached for the drinks to hand the next customers in line. The bright colors of the setting sun were fading, and in the dusky gloom, Sebastian again pulled over and unwrapped his seven-layer burrito. No sense in letting the food go to waste, he thought, chewing enthusiastically. Delicious! Not in the same league as his usual fare, but not bad at all. He just better not make this a new habit.

He mulled over what he had just learned. A man. It could be the new boyfriend of an ex, head full of stories and lies about Winston and having grandiose fantasies about beating up the ex-boyfriend to make himself look better. But if a guy was dating one of Winston's hot castoffs, why would they waste time spying on Winston? That didn't make sense at all.

He decided to call Winston and pass on the description on Bluetooth while driving home. Now that he had performed a legitimate errand and Winston was long gone, he could safely go back home and park in the garage. He would probably wait in the car while the garage door went down, just to be safe.

Winston picked up on the third ring. "Everything ok?"

"Yeah. In fact, I have a description for you."

"Great. Who was it? Or what did she look like?"

"Winston, it wasn't a she. It was a Caucasian male with dark hair, brown eyes, weathered skin, early thirties, and according to the perky teenager at the Taco Bell window, he was not very attractive."

"You're kidding. I wasn't expecting that. And is the unattractive dude still following you?"

"I think so, but I'm just going to go home."

"Ok, but you call me once you get safely inside. If you haven't called me in thirty minutes, I am going to call the police."

"Yes, Mommy. I mean, *sir*."

"Sebastian, I am serious. If it is Gary, he means business. And if he hates me enough to waste his time following my car all over fast-food hell, he may do something drastic."

"I think I have the upper hand just knowing he is there. He won't be able to sneak up on me anyway."

"That's true. Thanks, Sebastian. You are the best. I don't know what I ever did to deserve you."

"Well, you thank me handily every other Friday," Sebastian said, laughing. It felt good to ease the tension. He realized he had been white-knuckling the steering wheel but was starting to ease off. "Hey! I'm pretty sure the guy just realized I am heading home, so he took off."

"What a relief," Winston said. "Oh! Did you get his license plate number?"

Sebastian smacked his forehead. "What an idiot I am! No, Winston, I didn't. I'm sorry I blew that."

"My fault for not thinking of it sooner. Well, I'm at Allie's, and I haven't been able to spend any time talking to her yet, so now that I know you are safe, I'm going to go. Ok?"

Winston disconnected and went to find Allie.

"What was that all about?" she asked.

If he told her what he suspected, she wouldn't be able to function. "Nothing to worry about. Now, I think you were telling me about your new classes this semester? Do you think you can beat your grades last semester?"

"I think so, but my grades were pretty good." She grinned. "Not bad for a fourteen-year-old dropout, huh?"

"Not bad at all." He tucked an unruly lock of her hair behind her ear. "But it doesn't leave much room for improvement, though, does it?"

She shrugged. "I think I can be ok with the status quo," she quipped.

Winston didn't give the gray Ford a single thought as he drove home.

Chapter 29

A Sighting

"HAVE YOU SEEN THAT car again, Sebastian?" Winston asked a few days later. His routine of heading into the office, working on the Gerald Simpson case, going to lunch with one or both of his parents, and coming home pleasantly tired in the evenings kept him busy. He had vague plans of taking Allie to do something adventurous this coming weekend if her workload would allow it. Staying home on weekdays was previously unheard of, but he liked his new normal.

"The gray Ford? No, sir."

"Have you seen any car, for that matter?"

Sebastian hesitated. He had seen multiple cars of different makes and models parked in positions that had a good view of the house. Binoculars had revealed that, in those cars, there was indeed a man of the same description given him by the Taco Bell girl.

The silence spoke volumes. "Sebastian! Why have you not told me? I think it's time to call the police!"

"I didn't want to worry you. Things have gone splendidly for you at work, and I didn't want that to be interrupted by a . . . distraction. I will take care of it, sir."

Winston let out the breath he was holding. Sebastian had a point. He was already finding it difficult to concentrate at work since his evening with Allie. She invaded his thoughts constantly.

Allie had expressed growing fear and unease that Gary was after her. She told Winston about the news segment. Winston had gotten in the habit of recording the news since he'd helped Allie escape. He scrolled back to the night of the gala and was positively flabbergasted when he saw the clip of him and Allie. Why had he ever decided to take on that assignment and go to such a high-profile event? What had he been thinking? At this point, he had to tell Allie. She was right to be afraid.

And now he knew for sure that Gary was the one in the gray Ford. He would have to steer well clear of Allie so there was no way he would lead Gary to her.

He called Allie immediately.

"Winston, I know. I've been looking over my shoulder nonstop. I just have the creepiest feeling he is going to come after me. Do you think he will know I'm associated with you?"

"I'm afraid so," Winston answered. "I plan to stay away from you for a while. But it will be hard. "

"I'm worried about you. He is absolutely crazy. If he thinks I'm associated with you, you could be in real danger."

"Don't worry. I have Sebastian here at all times. If he tries to do something crazy, one of us will call the police."

Ever since her conversation with Daniel, a sense of unease had plagued her. Now Winston had confirmed her fears. She tossed and turned all night.

That morning, she prayed she would be kept safe, that Gary would not be able to find her or hurt Winston, and that she would find the peace and closure she needed. She prayed they would be able to find a solution Gary approved of and they could all find a way to be happy. She closed her prayer and grabbed a piece of toast for breakfast so she could eat on the way to class.

She was pleased and excited by the grade she received in her math class. All the hard work and struggle had been worth it. Ballet class was a welcome distraction, and she enjoyed every minute of it. Daniel found her and walked her to and from all her classes.

After she said goodbye to Daniel, she remembered she was out of shampoo and low on deodorant. She decided to make a brief detour on her way home and purchase a few things at Target. Her earlier apprehension was gone, replaced with a satisfying peace and the glow of happiness that usually came after ballet and anytime she relished her newfound freedom.

She tossed some Colgate into her cart. Suddenly, the hair on the back of her neck rose, and she refrained from looking around.

He was here.

She could feel it. But if he had already spotted her, he would be at her side already, holding her wrist in his signature death grip and whispering threats in her ear. Her heart thumped as she quietly looked for the nearest escape.

Escape.

She hadn't felt that heaviness, that foreboding, that sense of being trapped since the day Winston had rescued her at the beach. The way she had felt since then was such a severe contrast. She had learned to feel light and happy, safe and secure. She had laughed more in these past few weeks than in the many years she'd known Gary.

Now that she knew what happiness and freedom felt like, going back to her awful life with Gary would be worse than death. She could not let it happen.

She hunched over and threw her hood over her hair, hiding in plain sight. She deliberately changed the way she walked and controlled her telltale mannerisms. Her eyes scanned for an exit, but she disregarded the closest one, since it was devoid of people. She stayed in the thickest of the throng inside the store. She shivered inside the hoodie and stayed on the fringe of a large family group, leaving when they did and looking every bit like one of them. At her car, she put on her dark sunglasses and lowered her seat, searching for Gary, her heart beating fiercely.

Even though she had sensed his presence, when she spotted him, her stomach dropped like she was riding a plummeting roller coaster. His head swiveled, his eyes darting, urgently seeking as if he, too, had sensed Allie's presence. Allie shivered when he looked her way, his eyes scanning the parking lot. Why hadn't she left already? Would he go through the parking lot, peeking in every car? If she left now, would he note her license plate and track her down? Dread consumed her. Like stalked prey, she stayed still, trying to outlast him. Then, to her relief, Gary slipped away, his search to continue inside the store. Allie did not waste the window of opportunity. She pulled out and drove away, calling Winston as she did so.

"Hello." Winston's voice sounded cheerful and welcoming, and some of that warmth soothed Allie.

"I saw him. I saw Gary," she said, sounding hysterical even to her own ears.

"You did? Where? Did he see you?"

"I'm at Target at the huge shopping complex. He did not see me," she said. Then, in a quiet voice, low with anxiety, she added, "But I'm pretty sure he knew I was there. Winston, I have a bad feeling about all this. What are we going to do?"

"I think it might be time to go to the police. Share your story. Get them looking for him. At least let them know what his intentions are," Winston suggested.

Allie thought about it. "Can they make me go back to him?' she asked.

"No. Of course not," Winston soothed.

Again, Allie felt tremendous relief. She'd rather live constantly watching her back than return to Gary and the ranch. She would miss her freedom, but she would miss Winston most of all. An ache started just thinking of the dreadful possibility of never seeing Winston again. He made her life so full and happy.

"Ok, if you think it will help, I'll do it. Do you think they'll be mad when they realize how much time they wasted searching for me at the beach?"

"I think when we explain your story, they will fully understand. And you won't be going to the police station alone. I will be there. I will explain what I did and why I did it. And then you can explain that Gary is now looking for you. And I think he has been following me," Winston said, throwing in the craziness of the gray Ford.

～ ～

Allie felt good as they walked out of the police station. Really, the officers could not have been nicer or more understanding. Professionally, they'd hidden their initial shock at having a "dead woman" walk into the station. But as the story unfolded, they talked more and more about what they could do to help her. They would be on the lookout for Gary. They couldn't arrest him—not even for stalking—but if he made one wrong move, they would be after him.

Allie was still worried about what Gary's next move would be, but she felt much more secure knowing the law and good friends were on her side.

And she would not have to return to Gary.

Chapter 30 ———————————————————————————

Taking Action

THIS WASN'T WORKING.

Parked down the street, Gary watched the comings and goings, hoping for the glimpse of Alexandria that confirmed she was living there, but all the vehicles that pulled out of the garage were darkly tinted. He couldn't see a thing. No one seemed to use the front door. Impatient with his stakeout, he pulled his hat low and knocked on the door.

"Can I help you?" asked a cultured voice, a little reminiscent of Jeffery, the butler on the '90s sitcom *The Prince of Bel-Air*. With a start, Gary realized this must be an actual butler. Crazy.

"Can I speak to the lady of the house, please?" Gary asked politely.

The butler stared him up and down. "Sorry, no lady of the house. The man of the house is otherwise occupied. Can I help you?"

Gary thought quickly. What was something only a woman would be interested in? A rich one at that.

He cleared his throat. "I have developed a revolutionary workout regimen especially designed to help burn fat in key areas on a woman's body. It's so new and rare we are going door to door in exclusive neighborhoods." Gary was one slick salesman. "So, any women in the house?" he asked.

"Just a cook and housekeeper. I doubt they would want—or could afford—such a revolutionary program. Best of luck." Sebastian firmly closed the door.

Gary turned away, puzzled. Was she not there? Maybe he'd imagined the entire connection with this guy. Maybe she had been at that gala with someone else and just happened to be in the photo. Or maybe they were together, just not living together. But if that were the case, then surely this guy would have led him to her apartment by now. Well, he couldn't give up just yet. If she wasn't in the house now, maybe she would be later. He had to summon all of his patience. But, really, he wanted to scream because after following a lot of cars and ending up in fast-food drive-thru lines, Gary had had enough of patience. He was sick of sitting inside this car. He was sick of staring at the mansion. His rage was building.

It was time to act.

By 3:00 a.m., not even a dog was barking. All was dark. All was quiet. Silently, Gary opened and closed the car door behind him. He fingered the wrench set in his front pocket. He would scope out a back door first, but he would enter by the front door if he had to. He tried the front door just in case. Locked. He looked at all the windows. They were shut tight, probably running the AC, he thought. He wiggled a door near the garage. Also locked. He pulled out his set of tools and looked for the right fit, then started to pick the lock. Finally, he heard the click and went to pull it open, but it caught and wouldn't budge. Gary nearly kicked himself for not noticing the dead bolt. He moved on.

Gary stared at the tall iron fence that literally barred him from the backyard. Did he need a key for the gate too? The lock mechanism was complicated, but he soon figured it out and pushed the heavy door on smooth hinges. He couldn't believe his luck when he ascended the stairs to the deck and found the French door open. A flimsy screen door was all that stood between him and finding Alexandria if she was inside. The screen door was locked. Gary pocketed his tools and pulled a credit card out of his wallet, sliding it down until the metal latch was brushed aside. He paused with one foot inside and one outside for a quick getaway. He started when a grandfather clock proudly chimed the half hour. Then its ticking was the only audible sound.

He was in a vast room with couches, tables, a big screen on one side, and an enormous kitchen on the left, with barstools connected to a huge island. There were double fridges, double ovens, and double sinks. A modest dining room set that probably sat only ten paralleled a wall of windows. Through a tall archway, he spotted a staircase. He guessed the bedrooms must be upstairs. He tiptoed down the hallway to the vast marble foyer, then looked up through the gloom, his eyes slowly adjusting to the dimness. He could see the curving stairway and balcony and a couple of closed doors. The bedrooms? Were they occupied? He started to ascend the steps.

"Winston?"

Gary froze.

"Winston? Is that you? Is everything ok? Can I get you anything?"

Gary was torn with indecision. He didn't want to make a commotion. He just wanted to check and see if Alexandria was there and, if she was, only take back what was rightfully his. Who was attempting to interfere?

"I'm fine. Go back to bed," he whispered, hoping everyone's voice was the same when whispered.

Silence. Gary held his breath. Then, finally, a quiet answer came back. "Okay, then."

He waited while the silhouette retreated. But then the lights came on, and the man's eyes widened when he saw that the man he had been talking to was absolutely not Winston. The butler who had previously answered the door grabbed a candlestick and brandished the weapon. "Get out of the house now and nobody gets hurt," he bargained.

"I don't want anyone to get hurt," Gary said. "I just want my wife."

"Your wife!" The butler looked astonished. "Why would you think your wife was here?"

"I saw her on the news—standing next to that man you call Winston."

"She's not here," the butler said.

"Then where is she?"

Sebastian shrugged. He couldn't tell this man that. He would go over to Allie's and Jenna's right now, in the middle of the night, and drag poor Allie away. But if he didn't tell, he was probably going to suffer the consequences.

Sebastian decided to yell for Winston to lock his door and call the police. He looked up toward his bedroom door. That was the last thing he saw. Gary had taken the candlestick and bashed him over the head. Sebastian crumpled to the floor. Gary grabbed him under the arms and dragged him to a room behind him. Seeing that it was a bathroom, he locked it from the inside, shoved Sebastian inside, and closed the door. Still carrying the candlestick, Gary hurriedly tiptoed up the stairs, not bothering to turn off the downstairs light.

Most of the doors were shut, but not tightly. Gary slowly pushed them open. The furnishings were flashy, but the rooms were empty of sleeping occupants. He left what must be the master bedroom for last, then he went back downstairs, quickly scanning the other rooms. Fortunately, the cook and housekeeper must not live on the premises.

Everything was quiet and empty except for the one downstairs bathroom that would be occupied for several hours at least. Only the master bedroom was left. He stood outside the door. If this guy Winston was sleeping with his Alexandria, he would kill him.

He turned the knob and entered, hovering inside the doorway. He raised the candlestick, ready if necessary. Snoring. Heavy snoring. No Alexandria. Where was she? Had he made a mistake by knocking out the butler? That man obviously knew who he was and what he was talking about. Well, then so would this man. Here was a moment of decision: wake this guy up and demand answers or just walk away, pretending this entire thing was a burglary gone awry. But if he did that, the butler would remember him and identify him. Gary didn't want to have to kill him, but he would rather do that than alert Alexandria he was on her trail. Plus, how would that help him get her back? What should he do? What if he took Winston with him and demanded he show him where Alexandria was?

He went down to a storage room and found some rope and he grabbed a knife from the kitchen. Winston woke with a start as Gary roughly cinched the rope pinning his arms tightly behind his back.

"What the—?" Winston asked, alarmed but groggy.

He looked at Gary and immediately started struggling with the ropes. "It's you!" he managed to get out.

"Where is my wife?" Gary said, sounding scary and threatening even to his own ears.

Winston shook his head.

"Tell me!" Gary demanded.

"Sebastian! Sebastian! Help!" Winston yelled.

Gary threw his greasy head back, laughing. "Sebastian isn't going to be helping you anytime soon."

"What did you do to him? Is he ok?" Winston looked genuinely scared.

Gary thought it was better not to answer the question. Keep the man wondering, even thinking the worst, and maybe he would be more cooperative. Winston's eyes looked wild. "Where is she?" Gary asked again.

Winston just shook his head.

Gary pressed the knife to Winston's throat. "Either tell me now, or I'm going to cut your throat." A few tears leaked from the corners of Winston's eyes, but he bravely stared down his captor.

"Don't make me use this!" Gary shouted.

But again, Winston just shook his head.

Gary was so angry he used extra force when he bashed his second victim over the head.

Chapter 31 ————————————————————————————

The Chase

SEBASTIAN AWOKE TO A dragging sound, then a thump, thump, thump. Was Winston coming down the stairs? Sebastian felt a pounding in his head that echoed that strange thumping. What had happened? And then he remembered—Allie's ex-husband. That sound must be him dragging Winston down the stairs. Sebastian had to do something. With tremendous effort, he sat up. He was glad it was too dark to see everything spinning. Quietly, he got to his feet, lurching like a drunk and catching himself on the wall. He listened as the front door was unbolted and opened. He unlocked the bathroom door and staggered out. All was quiet.

Depending on how far away the man's car was, Sebastian could catch him and follow him. Unfortunately, in his concussed state, he didn't think clearly enough to grab his cell phone. He just reacted, stumbling to the garage to jump into Winston's sports car.

Gary had dumped Winston's body into the trunk and was opening the driver's side door when he heard the hum of a garage door being opened. A bright-red Porsche shot down the driveway and was coming right at him. Impossible, he thought. He'd knocked that guy over the head, hard. Oh, well, his driving—and his thinking—had to be impaired, Gary thought.

Rubber squealed as Gary stomped on the accelerator.

Sebastian pursued, gaining ground in the speedy sports car.

"Oh, why didn't I call the police?" Sebastian said out loud, groaning, his hands white-knuckling the steering wheel, his head feeling like it was about to explode.

"Why can't I shake him?" Gary complained through gritted teeth, weaving and dodging parked cars on the nearly deserted streets as he kept his eyes mostly on the rearview mirror and throwing in as many last-minute turns as possible.

Finally, Sebastian guessed he was headed to the interstate. He decided that rather than follow Gary, he would take a shortcut to the freeway entrance.

Gary rejoiced when the car disappeared from behind him, but he'd celebrated too soon. He cursed when the Porsche reappeared in front of him, blocking his way to the freeway. His rage boiled over. The Porsche was dead center on the crown of the overpass and could move either forward or back to block his way, depending on which way he tried to go around.

But escape was still possible, Gary thought. Maybe a quick U-turn and a different route. But the Porsche was faster, and for all Gary knew, the police could also be in pursuit. Maybe a hard crash would make that pesky butler black out, he thought.

Gary revved the engine, taking off with tires squealing. He could see the panicked face of the driver through the windshield as the heavy, clunky old car sped toward him. At the crown of the overpass, the impact of the heavy car at top speed caught the Porsche slightly underneath the bumper. Gary could scarcely believe his luck as he watched the car fly upward and sideways, landing on top of the guardrail, teetering precariously. Gary bashed into the Porsche again, backed up, then bashed into it again. The Porsche rocked a bit, then toppled.

Sebastian had blacked out on impact, his previous injuries making one more too much to handle. He was unaware as the Porsche plummeted nose-down into the asphalt below, crumpling the front of the car and them slamming back roughly onto the pavement, bouncing, then coming to a rest, its gleaming metal now looking like a jaggedly opened soup can.

Chapter 32

Missing

"THAT IS SO NOT true, and you know it!" Allie exclaimed, laughing as she rushed through the apartment door with Daniel on her heels.

"You just don't want to believe it," Daniel answered in a teasing voice.

Allie threw her backpack on the sofa, then whirled around when Jenna asked urgently, "Didn't you get my text?" Jenna's face was pale and drawn.

"Jenna! Are you ill? My phone was on silent. I forgot to unmute it after class. What's wrong?"

Jenna sank to the couch. She looked at Allie and Daniel gravely. "It's Winston. And Sebastian." Emotion welled up, and she couldn't continue.

Dread filled Allie. She sat beside Jenna and put an arm around her friend. "Tell me," she said softly.

"They were in a car accident. Well, at least Sebastian was. We don't know where Winston is," Jenna said.

Allie gasped. "Is Sebastian okay? Winston is missing?" Then realization dawned. "Gary! Gary did this! Tell me everything you know."

Jenna explained that when the housekeeper had come in that morning, the front door was wide open, the Porsche was gone, the garage door was also open, and Winston and Sebastian were gone. But the worst part was finding traces of blood in the hall near the stairs and more in the downstairs bathroom. She immediately called the police, and they told her they had an unidentified man who had been in a car accident. At first she thought it was Winston, but the description fit Sebastian.

"I'm calling the police too," Allie said. "This is all my fault. Winston has done nothing but help me, and now Sebastian is hurt and Winston could be too."

Rather than call, she drove to the police station. The officer's mustache itched with incredulity as Allie explained the entire story.

Allie didn't even notice. "So I believe Gary is responsible for the accident and for Winston's disappearance. Could you find a way to verify Gary's whereabouts?" she asked anxiously.

The policeman nodded gravely. "Let me make some phone calls. Excuse me," he said. He shuffled out of the room, glancing back at her as he exited.

"You will never guess who's sitting in my office," he said before the door had clicked all the way shut.

Allie sighed and pulled out her phone. Jenna was at the hospital with Sebastian and no news was forthcoming regarding Winston. Allie explained where she was and promised to get there as soon as she could.

"I am fine here, Allie," Jenna said. "I am so grateful you went to the police station. How long will it take them to find Winston?"

"I have no idea. Right now I think they are pursuing Gary as a lead and trying to track his whereabouts. If they find Gary, they may find Winston," Allie said.

"What if Gary is back in South Dakota and had nothing to do with what happened?"

Allie's heart went cold. "That's a possibility, I suppose. But I did see Gary a few days ago."

The door opened, and Allie jumped. She stood up, wringing her hands. "Did you find anything out?" she asked.

"I'm afraid not. No answer at the residence in South Dakota. No answer on that cell phone number you gave me. In fact, that number is no longer in service. And no answer at his parents' residence," he said.

"That surprises me," she said. "I don't think they leave the house much."

"We will keep checking. Maybe we will send somebody out there. For now, would you like to remain here? It could be dangerous for you if he is close by."

Allie hadn't thought she could get any tenser. She was wrong. But she told Jenna she was heading to the hospital and to call the police if she didn't show up soon. She looked around suspiciously as she walked to her car, as she drove, and as she headed into the hospital.

Allie wept at the hospital bedside. She held Sebastian's hand.

The doctor had said his chances were not very good. He had a lot of broken bones and internal bleeding. But he did have a chance. The doctor explained that Porsches were solid cars and the front of the car had absorbed most of the impact. The comfortable seat and seat belt had managed to cushion a lot of the blow.

Allie prayed harder for Sebastian than she had ever prayed, pleading with God to spare his life, to restore his health, to help his body recover quickly.

Jenna held her hand and prayed with her.

Then their prayers turned to Winston. Where was Winston?

Chapter 33 ———————————————————————

Gary's Prisoner

THE DOOR SLAMMED AS Gary walked in, and Winston felt a mixture of relief and fear. As awful as it was when Gary was around, the moments of silence and fear and uncertainty when he wasn't were equally as appalling.

The man was crazy. Insane. Obsessed with Alexandria. And he worked on gaining a psychological hold over Winston so that Winston would give away her whereabouts. Did they teach classes on being a psycho? Winston wondered.

The dinner smelled divine. Winston couldn't remember the last time he had eaten. The spaghetti steamed on the plate, a meatball precariously slipping across the marinara sauce from the top down to the side. A bread-stick steamed next to it.

"If you tell me where to find my wife," he said with menacing emphasis, "then this dinner is all yours. If not, it's seconds for me."

Arms tied to the armrests of the swivel chair, Winston watched help-lessly. He thought through the scenarios. If he didn't answer, Allie would stay free and he wouldn't eat, and this pattern would repeat until he got hungrier and weaker. Maybe he would eventually starve to death. If he did answer, he would eat, but then Gary wouldn't need him anymore and would probably kill him. Neither of those scenarios was especially appeal-ing, but he had to protect Allie. If he told a lie, however, then he could eat and it would bide him some time to think of a new plan and Allie would be safe. But then Gary would probably be so mad he would kill Winston. He couldn't see a way out that would preserve his life *and* keep Allie safe.

But maybe if he did buy some time, the police could somehow locate him. He thought of the address to his old apartment and hoped the guys who lived in there now worked out or knew karate or something. He needed to pretend to be torn up about divulging Allie's address. When Gary came back angry, he could always say he'd made a mistake. And if he did share Allie's real address, then surely she would be on the lookout for Gary or even have police protection, right?

Winston didn't know what to do. It seemed like every choice was the wrong one. But the spaghetti smelled really good.

Staring at the food and acting reluctant, he told Gary, "Okay, okay, I'll talk. But you can't hurt her. And if I tell you, will you please let me go?"

Gary's cold, dark eyes studied Winston. "Eventually," he said. He cracked a couple of knuckles, the sound echoing off the dark, hard walls. Winston shivered. This place was damp and cold and had a weird feeling about it. Where was he? The single naked light bulb barely lit the large cavernous room. Either it was night or the room didn't have any windows. Winston was too disoriented to know which, and he hadn't seen much. He had been drugged and in a deep sleep most of the time. When he awoke the first time, he was on a sleeping bag on the floor with only a bucket for a toilet. When he woke the second time, he was tied to a chair, unable to reach the food. This was the second time Gary had tempted him with food to divulge Allie's whereabouts.

"What do you mean, eventually?" Winston asked.

"When I get her back and we are safely away, I will call someone and tell them where to find you," he said, shrugging.

"And where am I?" Winston asked.

Gary smiled, but it made his unattractive face even less attractive. "Somewhere no one will ever find you," he said. "So what is the address? The sooner you tell me, the sooner we can quit playing this fun little game. Though I was just starting to enjoy myself."

He is growing even more psycho, Winston thought, starting to panic. What should he do? He still felt his best option was to send the guy to his old apartment, but it was awfully close to the truth since it, too, was close to campus.

"Ok. She lives at 430 Cedar Park. It's an apartment. She's in number 2024," he said.

Gary's Prisoner

"If you're lying to me, there will be severe consequences," he bellowed.

How does he know what I'm thinking? Winston wondered. Allie had warned him of his uncanny intelligence. Should he rethink his plan or take his chances? "If you hurt her, there will be consequences," Winston bellowed back.

Gary arched a brow. "Oh? So you like *my wife*, do you?" he spat out possessively.

Winston did not dare admit how much he truly had grown to love and care for Allie, but he felt the impact of that love in his heart. This crazy psycho, this monster in front of him, didn't deserve such a wife. And truly, without coercion, he never would have made her his wife. With wonder and astonishment, he realized that not only had Allie managed to survive being married to this man, abused and isolated as she was, she had come out of it stronger, smarter, more remarkable, and more resilient. Allie had managed to learn to love and care about others and grow and thrive both in and out of this man's presence. Winston had renewed respect for Allie.

"Whether I like her or not is irrelevant," Winston answered. "What matters is that a true man never hurts a woman. *Ever.*"

Gary recoiled as if he had been struck. "I have been around animals all my life. When they misbehave, you strike them. They don't misbehave again," he said coldly.

Winston's eyes widened. "You don't mean what I think you mean," he said incredulously.

Gary nodded, unblinking with those chilly eyes.

Winston said, "Well, you have grossly misbehaved. Who's going to take the whip to *you*?"

Gary came over and slapped Winston across the face, knocking the chair over, Winston's face pressed into the ground. Gary laughed cruelly. "Well, I got what I came for," he said. "And I never made any promises about anything else. But I will at least untie you. I wouldn't want you to make any more of a mess of yourself than you already have. He cut the ropes on Winston's wrists, not caring that he'd also nicked skin in the process. The door closed with a solid slam and the clicking of the lock.

Winston stumbled to his feet and searched the room for a way out. The walls were solid. He was in a cement basement. He looked at the ceiling. Maybe he could use the chair to break through the ceiling. He searched the room, but he had only the chair, the bucket, and the dinner. Deciding the food could give him a bit of strength, he ate quickly, turned the bucket over to stand on, and began slashing at the ceiling with the chair. Winston had barely managed to chip away at the ceiling, but he was exhausted. It was just too far out of reach, and gravity didn't work in his favor as he tried to hurl the chair at it.

Winston sat quietly for a long time, the emptiness of time stretching before him. His thoughts turned to Allie. He was powerless to help her. What would Allie do in this situation? She would pray, he realized. When she had been powerless before, she had turned to prayer. Now, he was the one who was completely powerless. For a long time, he thought about what he wanted to say in his prayer.

"Please, God," he pleaded, dropping to his knees as he began to pray. "Please help her. Keep her safe. I love her, Lord. I love her, and I need her. I think she needs me too. I promise to take good care of her. I've tried to take good care of her but also allow her to grow into the person she's meant to be. I have tried to do everything right for her, but I have failed. I was not able to keep her safe. But you, God, I know you can do all things. You can keep her safe. Please protect her. Please forgive me for my shortcomings. I have been prideful. I have not turned to you. But I am ready to turn to you now. Please. For Allie. Please protect Allie."

Winston's tears dropped faster than rain during a deluge. He had to collect himself and try again.

"Dear God in heaven," Winston prayed. "I believe you are there. I have believed you were there since something greater than I was told me that I needed to help Allie. Thank you—" Unexpectedly, he choked up with emotion. "Thank you for choosing me to be the answer to Allie's prayer. I know I was not worthy to be chosen, but I want you to know I'm working on that. Since Allie has come into my life, I've wanted to be better, to be worthy to stand in the presence of one who is so pure. I have desires to develop the kind of faith Allie has so that one day I might be worthy to have my prayers answered. So God in heaven, since I am still not worthy to have my prayer answered of being delivered out of this situation, will you please hear my pleading on Allie's behalf? Will you please keep her safe and far away from this awful husband of hers? If anything happens to me, will you see to it that my parents take care of Allie and her needs, that they keep her safe?"

His hands were clasped, and big, drenching tears continued to cascade down his cheeks as he pleaded for Allie's welfare. "God, I love Allie. I'm so thankful she came into my life. I'm thankful for my parents and that my relationship with them has been restored. I am grateful Allie brought me to you. If I do live, help me to know you better and to be worthy of Allie and her love." He closed his prayer in Jesus's name and stayed on his knees, hands clasped, feeling the Spirit wash over him, reassuring and comforting him.

And somehow he knew Allie was going to be all right. He could see the big picture. He could see that Allie had come into his life, basically as an on-the-earth angel, to help him change and grow and to mold him into the person he was becoming. God had answered Allie's prayer and lifted her out of a hurtful, abusive situation and into one where Winston was able to help her, care for her, and also help her grow into the person she was meant to become. Winston marveled at God's goodness, grace, and mercy. He marveled he had played a role in helping Allie. He marveled at how much had changed in both of their lives since that fateful day at the beach.

Somehow, while he was helping Allie to grow and change, the same thing had happened to him. His life, his wants, and his desires were completely different than they had been before Allie came into his life.

He almost laughed out loud at the irresponsible party-going, surfer dude who had been transformed into someone who would rather help Allie study on a Friday night or work on one of his cases than go to the club with Tessa and the girls. His desires to go from one adventure to the next had been replaced with the desire to work hard, help others, get married, and have a family. If the situation wasn't so dire, he would have lamented that he was turning into his father! But now, from his new perspective, he realized that wasn't a bad thing to be. He had the utmost respect for his father. He had an amazing work ethic. He used to think his father was driven by greed and money and ambition, but he could see the truth. His father was a good-hearted man who cared about his family. He cared about justice and the law. He cared about doing his best. He enjoyed using his brains to solve problems and help others. Winston admired him. His father had sacrificed a lot of his own worldly pleasures so that his wife and children could enjoy them. Now, Winston couldn't think of anything nobler than to follow in his father's footsteps.

But to do that, he had to get out of here. And he would do that. His heart filled with hope. Although he knew his prayer might not be answered, he had faith that Allie's prayer would.

Chapter 34 ————————————————————————————

The Cave

ALLIE FOLLOWED THE POLICE car and waited down the street while the police went to investigate Gary's parents' house. The door opened, and the officers disappeared inside. As the minutes ticked slowly by, Allie began to pray the officers would find Winston in there—or at least Gary, who could then lead them to Winston. She prayed Winston would be all right. She prayed Winston's parents would have the strength they needed to endure this hardship.

The door opened, and the officers emerged, smiling graciously. When the door closed, Allie put on her sunglasses and went to ask what had happened.

One of the officers said, "They saw Gary a few days ago. He said he had heard you were still alive and that he came to get you back. But they haven't seen him since. They were concerned about you and wondered if he had found you. I told them you were all right but gave them no details. This was a dead end. But don't worry. We'll find him. I'm going to report in and get back to work," he said, striding quickly to his patrol car, where he got in, made a U-turn, and sped away.

Allie sighed and surveyed the neighborhood as she debated what to do. Should she knock on the door and talk to Gary's parents? Should she tell them her side of the story without Gary present? Somehow, she didn't think that would do any good. She had long suspected they had abused Gary like he'd abused her. She was better off staying away from them.

She walked back to her car, observing the well-kept, nice homes in the neighborhood. They were tucked into a private area backed against a small hill typical of the rugged California landscape. This was an extremely beautiful neighborhood. Her in-laws must have received a sizable payment for their enormous ranch. The hilly area behind the neighborhood had lots of sagebrush and very few trees. Her breath caught when she noticed a ribbon of water cutting its way through the bottom of a ravine. Homes dotted the nearby hills, but there was a lot of space in between them. Gary could have set up a tent down by the river and remained unseen. But unless Winston was gagged, he could call for help, and someone was sure to hear him. She didn't think Gary could be hiding him here. Or could he?

Taking advantage of her solitude, Allie knelt on the ground near her car.

"Dear God. I know you are there. I know you have helped me, and I am so grateful. You answered my prayers through Winston. He has helped me to start a new life and to be happy. Because of him, I have friends, and I'm getting an education. I even feel like I have new parents because his parents have been so good to me. I owe Winston everything. So now I want to be the answer to his prayers. Is he praying?" she asked aloud. Deep within, she felt he was. Over the last few weeks, he had shown more interest in the faith that had kept Allie going through her hardships. She closed her eyes and continued. "Please, God. Please give me the inspiration to find him. I will look everywhere. I will put in the effort if you will guide me. I know you know everything. I know you love Winston. Please help me find him."

She closed her prayer and stayed quietly kneeling. Back when she lived with Gary, in her quietest moments of despair, she had felt the whisperings of the Holy Spirit speaking words of comfort. They were silent yet audible to her mind. Now, in similar circumstances, she waited, hopeful and listening yet determined to do her part in the search. Just as people were often the means of answering prayers for one another, people and their efforts were also the means of answering prayers for themselves.

She wandered the entire hillside, which she realized wasn't very smart under the circumstances, and then dropped into the ravine. She called out to Winston. She hoped maybe he was being held in a small shelter, like a tent, shack, or an abandoned kid's fort. Among the sparse trees, however, she felt she would have spotted one if it existed.

Gary would not know this area well. Maybe she needed to look for more obvious hiding places that wouldn't take a long time to find. Near the river running through the bottom of the ravine, she spotted what looked like a cave. Her spirits rose. This had to be the place! In her haste to reach the cave, her feet slipped on some loose rocks. Unable to regain her footing, she came dangerously close to toppling into the water. Now, perched precariously on the lip of a slight overhang above the water, she was grateful she had caught herself in time. What if Gary was in the cave and had heard a splash? She would be soaked and helpless—and at Gary's mercy.

And she knew firsthand that there was no such thing as Gary's mercy.

She looked down, expecting to see the bottom of the creek. It looked deep right here, but upon closer inspection, she could see rocks and boulders jutting out from shallower places in the water.

Slowly, she clawed her way up from the ravine and silently made her way to the cave. She debated whether to call the police or investigate. What if Gary was in there and he grabbed her?

She pulled out her cell phone and checked for a signal. She had service. She sent a quick text to Jenna. "I'm looking for Winston. I'm going to check out a cave near the creek at the bottom of the ravine south of Gary's parents' house. If I don't text you back in fifteen minutes or less, please call the police!"

She waited for a response. If Jenna didn't answer, she would try Daniel next. But Jenna did answer. "Be careful!"

Allie sucked in a deep breath and stealthily approached the cave. She poked her head inside. Her eyes adjusted, and she could see the sides of the cave, though nothing in the darkness beyond. Halfway in and halfway out, she listened intently. She hoped to hear any indication that Winston might be there. She kept her fingers crossed that it would only be Winston. Her hands gingerly felt for the wall of the cave and used it as a guide. Did she dare use a light? How many minutes had gone by? Should she send Jenna another text, extending her time? This cave might be connected to tunnels that could take a long time to explore. She had moved far enough away from the entrance that the light was extremely dim. The ceiling was getting lower and lower. She had to crouch down, and soon she might be crawling. The stillness was unsettling—not even a whisper of wind or a bird chirp from outside. Her breath echoed off the cramped walls, making her sound like Darth Vader. She held her breath and listened intently.

Not a sound. Feeling safe for the moment, she activated the flashlight on her phone and shone it around, the light casting eerie shadows on the jagged earthen walls. The entrance wasn't very far behind her, but she could now see a sharp bend in the tunnel ahead. She looked for an offshoot, but there wasn't one. The cave ceiling was lower and narrower on the opposite side. Ahead of her, it looked like it might be widening. She shone the light on the ground. If she could see footprints, she would know she was on the right track, but the ground looked undisturbed. She pressed her boot into the ground and pulled it back, revealing a faint mark. She looked for other footprints but didn't see any. Still, she inched her way through the darkness.

Then she bumped her head. "Ouch!" she yelled. "Ouch! Ouch! Ouch!" The echo was loud. She froze in fear, the pain in her head completely unacknowledged. She reached up and could feel the protrusion hanging from the ceiling. She brought the light up. While she was staring at the ground, the cave had come to an end. If she hadn't bumped her head, she would have slammed face-first into the back wall. She backed up and shone the light all around her.

The cave was empty.

She felt both relieved and disappointed. Winston wasn't in this cold, awful cave. But she still didn't know where he was. As quickly as possible, she scooted out of the cave and texted Jenna. "Don't call the police. I'm ok. Cave empty."

"What a relief!" Jenna answered immediately. "I'm on my way to the neighborhood to join you."

"What a relief," Allie texted back. "Thanks!"

From the cave, Allie walked to the water, curious how deep and wide it was. In some places it was super shallow, in others quite deep. She followed the water for a while but didn't see any more caves or hiding places. It just seemed like it would be convenient and helpful to hide near a water source, she thought.

She circled around, still searching as she made her way closer to the homes in the neighborhood on her way to meet Jenna.

The police were investigating and looking for Gary, and now Jenna was helping with the search. Allie was glad she was not on her own. In her gut, she knew they would find Winston. She had to hold on to that and keep looking.

Jenna gave a small cry when she saw Allie. "What happened? We need to get you doctored up."

Allie gently touched her head and winced. Her fingers came back wet and sticky. "I bumped my head pretty hard in the cave, but I didn't realize it was bleeding," she admitted.

Like a Boy Scout, Jenna was prepared. She pulled out her tiny first-aid kit and opened a cleansing wipe. Then she butterflied the wound closed.

"So now what?" Jenna asked, puzzled. "Do you still feel like Gary would be here somewhere close to his parents?"

Allie nodded, ignoring the headache that had blossomed. "It makes the most sense," she said. "He won't be very familiar with the area, so it just seems logical that he would be holding Winston nearby."

"Are you sure Winston is alive?"

Allie wasn't sure, but she felt like he was. She couldn't handle the alternative. It was just too awful. "I do. Do you?" She hated that her voice quivered with so much emotion.

But Jenna felt it too. Her own eyes watered when she answered with a soft yes.

"On foot or in a car?"

"I don't know." Allie was starting to feel the letdown from not discovering Winston in the cave. She couldn't lose faith and hope now, though. "Let's drive. We can cover more ground that way. But maybe we should go slowly, like we're on foot."

"Agreed. So I'm thinking we are looking for any property that might not have the currently-lived-in look. These are all nice homes, but some could be second homes where the owners keep them maintained but don't live in them most of the time."

"Brilliant," Allie said. "I'll look on my side of the street. Do you feel comfortable driving and looking on your side?"

"At this speed? Yes."

They puttered along. Jenna pulled over at one point so a lone car could go around them. All the houses on Gary's parents' street looked occupied. Same with the next street. And the next.

On the next street, however, one of the homes had a lawn that looked as if it had not been mowed in weeks. The window blinds were drawn. Allie pointed at it. "What do you think? Should we give that house a try?" she asked.

Jenna nodded. "One of us should stay here so we can call the police in case Gary is in there," she suggested. "I'll go."

"No. I'll go. You don't even know what Gary looks like," Allie said grimly.

Heart pounding, Allie approached the door, knocked, and waited. Nothing. She rang the doorbell. Still nothing. Now what? Should she try to look in a window? Just then, the door opened and an elderly gentleman poked his head out. "Can I help you?" he asked.

Startled and relieved, Allie blurted out the first thought that came into her head. "Hello, sir, I was just wondering if I could help out with mowing your lawn?"

The man chuckled. "It looks pretty frightful, doesn't it? My grandson was off to a Scout jamboree, but he should be able to mow it tomorrow. Thanks for the offer, though."

Allie made a bit of polite small talk before rejoining Jenna at the car. Another dead end.

Allie was getting very discouraged. What was Winston suffering right now? What was Gary doing to him? She shuddered. Every image that popped into her mind made her shiver. Jenna noticed and turned up the heat. The sun was dipping low in the sky. The large shade trees blocked the remaining sun rays and made the street seem gloomy. Allie rested her head in her hand and continued to stare out the window. A large shadow blocked even more of the sun. Allie stretched her neck to look up at the spire of the large corner church. They had worked their way out of the neighborhood and to the main road. The old stone church stood alone, set far back from the corner, its spire an impressive sight.

They looked at each other. "Are you thinking what I'm thinking?" Jenna asked.

"If you're thinking that huge, creepy church is where Gary is hiding Winston, then, yes, I'm thinking what you're thinking."

Chapter 35 ———————————————

Investigating

JENNA PULLED INTO THE lot. "Let's go investigate," she said, about to switch off the ignition.

"Actually, I think we might be better off hiding the car and walking a bit. If this is the place and Gary comes back, we don't want to tip him off that we're here."

"Good idea. You're much better at this Nancy Drew stuff than I am," Jenna said. Her attempt at a joke fell flat. They were both too nervous for humor. Jenna pulled out and parked across the street, midway between two houses. They got out and locked the door.

"What if it's locked?" Allie asked.

Jenna shrugged. "Don't they usually leave churches unlocked?"

The main doors were locked. A side entrance was also locked. They walked around to the back. Allie noticed a couple of window wells. "Hey, look! This place even has a basement. I think this location is a major possibility. It's close to Gary's parents' house, it's large, probably only used on Sundays, and it's in a fairly secluded location."

"I agree."

Allie's heart pounded with excitement. What if they found Winston?

Jenna suggested, "Let's try the windows. Or maybe we should tell the police and they can stake out this place."

"Well, what if that happens but Gary catches on and just doesn't come back for Winston but leaves him here to die?"

"You're right. And I don't think he should stay here a moment more than he has to."

Every window was locked. "We might have to break a window," Allie said, looking around for a large rock.

"Or we could call the pastor of this church to open it up for us, " Jenna suggested.

"That's a great idea."

They googled the name of the church online and called the number. After the fifth ring, the answering machine picked up. "Hello, this is Pastor Newland at the West Haven Church on Rycart Avenue. You have reached the office after hours. Please leave your name and number, and I will call you back." The machine beeped, and Allie left her name and cell phone number.

"I wonder if he checks that every day. Should we wait for a call back? Break in? Call the police?" Allie shuffled her feet, antsy with indecision.

"Do you really think he is here?" Jenna asked.

They looked at each other. The truth was, Winston could be anywhere, and the likelihood of him being here was not very high. They could be wasting precious time on what was possibly another dead end.

Maybe Gary had thrown Winston in his car and driven him to the ranch in South Dakota. Winston had been missing forty-six hours now, gone without a trace. The police had not found either Gary or his car. Gary's parents had not seen Gary for close to seventy hours. Allie thought it odd that if Winston was missing and out of the picture, why had Gary not come after her?

"I just had a thought," Allie said. "What if Gary has Winston in his car and is driving back to South Dakota?"

"That's actually pretty brilliant," Jenna said. "He would get Winston clear out of the way first, and then nab *you*. That would explain why he hasn't already come after you."

"That's what I was thinking too. So what should we do? Call the police in South Dakota to go check it out?"

"Yes. I think we will have to explain the entire situation. Do you think Gary has already biased the police against you, though?"

"I would place a major bet on that. One of the guys Gary went to high school with works on the police force. I think they got together for a beer once in a while."

Jenna groaned. "That guy is everywhere," she said, and Allie nodded. "Don't you have anyone you can call?"

"Not a soul," Allie admitted sadly. "My parents and brother are dead. I haven't seen most of my classmates since eighth grade, and the couple of friends I did have, well, Gary got to them, worked his evil magic, and basically convinced them I'm crazy."

Jenna had been told all this before, but in her jealousy, she had forgotten it. *Poor girl*, she thought, *she deserves all the happiness she can get.* I won't stand in her way anymore. If we get out of this, she can have both Winston and Daniel.

"What about your pastor?" Jenna asked.

"My pastor? Hmmm." Allie considered it. "That's a possibility. I didn't get to go to church the last couple of years, but my mother and I used to go all the time. And as far as I knew, Gary didn't set foot inside of a church."

She looked online and dialed the number. The pastor was friendly and asked how she was doing. She wished she would have decided how much to disclose before she'd made the phone call. He acted like he didn't know she had been missing, so she decided to only tell the basics.

"I'm worried about Gary," she said. "I'm out of town, and I don't know where Gary is. Would you be willing to go check on him? And would you please not let him know I asked you to go?"

"It's time I made an official visit to the ranch anyway. I've put it off far too long."

"It's not exactly conveniently located."

Pastor Martin chuckled.

"But I would be very grateful if you would go," Allie said. She held her breath, hoping he would go immediately. The silence was telling.

"I better go right away and set your mind at ease, shouldn't I?"

"I would appreciate it. I am really worried."

Allie hung up and turned to Jenna. They decided to get back in the car and drive around, looking for other places Gary could be hiding Winston while they waited for the pastor—both pastors—to call back. Allie told Jenna it would take him about fifteen minutes to drive out to the ranch, but then she realized the roads could be snowy and it could take twice that long.

"Would you mind terribly if I said a prayer?" Allie asked. "Look at my hands." They were trembling fiercely.

Jenna reached out with a warm, steadying hand and held Allie's. "You poor thing. You are worried sick. I would be grateful to have you pray."

She bowed her head and grasped Jenna's hand. "Dear God, I am grateful to have Jenna here to comfort and help me. I am grateful for Winston and for all he did to help me. I am grateful for Pastor Martin and his kindness in helping me just now. Please watch over and protect him—especially if Gary is there. Please let him find Winston if Winston is there alone. Please bless Jenna and me with inspiration and guidance if there is more we should be doing here."

She closed her prayer, and they both said amen.

"While you were praying I just realized what a good thing it was not to tell the pastor why you were looking for Gary. If he knew more, he might look for Winston or act suspiciously. That would tip Gary off that you sent him instead of it just being a random visit."

"Yeah, this way he will go as a complete innocent. He will have no reason to act suspiciously. He can just do his pastor thing," Allie said.

Jenna hugged her. Then she started the car, and they drove around. The time ticked by slowly. Neither had the heart for conversation. What was Winston doing right now? Where was he? Had the pastor arrived at the ranch yet?

The pastor called about the time they had given up on hearing from him. "Alexandria, I did make it to the ranch. No lights on in the house. I went to the bunkhouse and talked to a man named Sam. He said Gary went to California to visit his parents not quite a week ago and he hasn't seen him since."

"Thanks so much, Pastor Martin. Did you by chance ask Sam to call you when Gary got back?"

"I didn't. But I haven't left the ranch yet. I will pop my head in and ask him to do just that. I did, however, already invite him to church, and he said he would try to make it this Sunday. He confirmed the time and everything." The pastor chuckled, obviously pleased with himself. Allie thanked him, asked him to call if he heard from Sam or saw Gary himself, and then she hung up.

"Now what? We can't just call it a night. Poor Winston!"

"But maybe they are still driving to South Dakota," Jenna pointed out.

Allie shook her head. "I don't think so, and here is why: Let's say he had Winston tied up in the trunk. If he stopped for any length of time, Winston might manage to untie himself and escape. I don't think he would stop at a hotel. As it stands, he would have to go to gas stations that either blare loud music and are super noisy or empty. Even stopping for a few minutes could be difficult. He might pull over in some abandoned areas to sleep or even to let Winston out to use the restroom."

"Poor Winston! How miserable! Do you really think he's locked in Gary's trunk?"

Allie's eyebrows drew together as she thought about it. "I don't think so. My point was, if he decided to go to South Dakota, I think he would already be there by now. He would have driven straight through with as few stops as possible."

"That makes sense," Jenna agreed. "But that would still mean he is hiding somewhere around here, right?"

"I think so. Gary is just so unpredictable. I really thought he would have come after me by now. In fact, maybe he is trying to come after me, but Winston is protecting me by not telling Gary where to find me. We better not stay at our apartment anymore so that not even Winston knows where we are. I want Winston to tell Gary so he doesn't have to suffer whatever Gary might be doing to torture him. Poor Winston!"

"I already warned Sailor and Katie that our apartment might not be safe. But we have all been invited to stay at the Grovers'. The place is swarming with people, so it will be safe. If Gary shows up at our apartment, nobody will be there," Jenna said.

"But if Gary can't find us, how are we supposed to find Winston?" Allie asked.

Jenna thought about it. "Well, maybe taking Winston is like a trap," she said. "You go looking for Winston, you stumble right into his evil lair."

"That sounds straight out of scripted fiction, but evil lair also sounds like exactly the kind of place Gary would be waiting," Allie said.

They drove by the West Haven church one more time.

"I just feel like that could be Gary's evil lair," Allie said, staring at the solid stone edifice and gothic spires once again. "I wish we would have broken a window and explored it instead of waiting for the pastor to call us back."

"We still could," Jenna said, although the thought made her nervous. She bit her fingernail, a dirty habit she had not indulged in since seventh grade.

"You're exhausted," Allie said. "You've been at Sebastian's bedside non-stop since the wee hours yesterday and then you helped me all afternoon. Let's get you home to bed."

"Ok, but, remember, home for the next little while is Winston's parents' house until Gary and Winston are found."

"Oh, that's right," Allie said, remembering with a surge of gratitude Jonathan's foresight and thoughtfulness. What if Gary found their apartment—especially while she and her roommates were all there? She shivered at the onslaught of awful thoughts.

Sailor and Katie were already at the Grover's when they arrived and hugged Jenna and Allie as they walked through the doors. They were disappointed they didn't have any news.

That night, Jenna thought about it. What could she do? What if she were the one to approach Gary for information? She could pretend she'd seen him on the news and sympathized with his plight. She would try it in the morning.

Chapter 36 ———————————————————————

Jenna's Plan

Jenna knocked on the Tacklemans' door and asked if Gary was there. He was not, but she was invited in on the pretense that she was there to help. She asked to hear the entire story, all the while pretending to be on Gary's side. Maybe his parents had also been lying to the police and knew more than they were telling. Unfortunately, she didn't learn anything new.

"So what brings you to California?" Jenna asked.

"The weather. I've been biding my time, putting up with my arthritis until the time was finally right to retire and sell the ranch. We figured we'd either settle here or in Arizona. And when this was advertised with a protected river and ravine right behind it to ensure no large conglomerate was going to come in and throw up a mess of cheap houses behind us, we jumped at the opportunity."

"Well, it seems like a lovely home and great location. But again, I'm so sorry for what has happened with your daughter-in-law. It's a tragic circumstance," Jenna sympathized.

"Yes, tragic," Mrs. Tackleman agreed. "We have been hoping and waiting for grandchildren. Now, who knows when we will get some?" She sighed loudly.

"That's a big loss in itself," Jenna agreed. "And I'm sure your son is beside himself with grief."

"I've never seen him act like this before," his mother answered. "Oh, why did Alexandria insist on going to the beach that day? What a selfish, irresponsible, self-centered thing to do. And now we are all suffering the consequences."

Jenna nodded. "So you haven't seen Gary in days? Any idea where he is?" she asked.

Neither had a clue and started conversations on various tangents. So much for this plan, Jenna thought. At the first possible moment, she would make her excuses and head back to the hospital to visit Sebastian. Oh, well, it was worth a try. At least she wasn't sitting around doing nothing.

❧ ❧

Allie had her own agenda that morning. She couldn't stop thinking about that church. She checked her phone for a message from the pastor. When nothing was there, she drove straight to the police station. She explained why she thought it was a strong possibility that Winston could be held captive there.

"It wouldn't hurt to check it out, Jim," the lieutenant said. "Go ahead and go on out there."

"I'd like to come," Allie said. "Can I ride with you, or should I take my own car?"

"You better take your own car in case I get called out on another call," he said.

Allie gratefully followed behind. She felt much safer going into the church with an armed officer than if she and Jenna had tried to break in on their own. In fact, they probably wouldn't have been any safer with a crusty, old pastor. It was such a crusty, old church, she just assumed it had a crusty, old pastor to go with it, she thought guiltily.

The officer had a set of keys to the church, and with permission, they explored the entire building, from the chapel with its vaulted ceilings to the cramped spaces in the attic. But Allie insisted they search the basement. Every room was empty except for a few random broken pews and a closet stuffed with brooms, mops, and an assortment of cleaning supplies. Even the kitchen was devoid of almost everything except a few dented cake and cupcake pans and a ramshackle assortment of silverware and serving utensils.

"I don't think this church has been used in a while," the officer commented.

"Which makes it a perfect place to hide Winston," Allie answered.

But her discouragement mounted with each empty room. She had felt so certain Winston would be here. She wanted to cry. After her prayers last night and all through her restless dreams, she kept thinking of this church and knew she had to get in and find Winston. Could there be a secret room? But neither she nor the officer could find one. They searched. They called for Winston. They listened. All was still and quiet. Allie had to face facts: Winston was not here.

She thanked the officer for his time, then drove back to the hospital to visit Sebastian. He was awake and greatly improved. Allie talked with him until he visibly tired out. She didn't dare ask him anything about the night Winston disappeared.

But she did not stop praying.

Allie called and asked Jonathan if he could get access to various cameras through his connections with the police to try and track Gary down. Or maybe Jonathan had access to tracing credit cards? They could find out which state Gary was in and completely rule out a trip to South Dakota. Then they could narrow their search for Winston.

They were willing to try about anything.

Chapter 37 ——————————————————————————

Outsmarting

GARY CONSIDERED HIMSELF SUPER lucky when he saw a car and a couple of people snooping around the church. His luck continued when they gave up and left. If they hadn't, they might have discovered Winston. And if they had discovered Winston, he would have two more prisoners to deal with, so they were just as lucky as he was, he thought.

As soon as the coast was clear, he went in and removed Winston. But where to take him? He couldn't go to his parents' house anymore. It would certainly be under surveillance. But he could go to a hotel. Fortunately, he only had to hide Winston for a few hours. And even more fortunate, he had the horse tranquilizers with him and was able to knock Winston out for hours. People were a lot more cooperative when they were knocked out, Gary decided.

While Winston lay oblivious at a nearby Motel 6, Gary watched the church from a distance. Just as he suspected, a cop came to investigate. And was that Alexandria with him? He wished he hadn't left his binoculars at his parents' house. If the woman who looked like his wife weren't with a cop, he would snatch her right now and let the maids deal with his drugged guest tomorrow morning. But who knew what the cop would do. Better not risk it.

The cop and the woman talked for a minute, and then both drove away. Should he follow the woman and see if it was Alexandria? Were they searching for his captive, or was it an unrelated matter? Gary had no idea.

He looked at his watch. It was almost check-out time at the motel, and he didn't want to be charged for another night and use more of his precious cash. He decided to retrieve Winston and return him to his cell at the church. After the cop found it empty, he wouldn't be back. Winston wouldn't even know he had left his prison.

∽ ∼

Allie drove away from the hospital in a trance. The more time that passed, the more she worried. She prayed so hard. Why did she keep seeing that room in the church? The place had been empty. She had seen it with her own eyes. She drove over to where the road ended near the ravine and got out, finding a quiet place to pray.

"Dear God, please help me find Winston. He has been so good and kind to me. Please help me find him," she pleaded. She stayed on her knees with her hands clasped, waiting for that familiar feeling of love and comfort to wash over her. She had been blessed to make so many friends while she lived here, but she had not forgotten her first and only Friend. She prayed every night, thanking God for watching over for her and for answering her most sincere desire to be free of Gary. She prayed, thanking Him for Jenna, Sailor, and Daniel. She thanked Him for Winston's parents and their kindness.

She felt blessed beyond measure and so grateful she had turned to God in her great need. He was there for her then. She knew He was here for her now. She knew He was there for Winston. She closed her eyes. Again, she saw that dark room in the church, the one that seemed like a stone jail cell. She had shivered the first time she walked into that empty room. Suddenly, she remembered how it did not have a stale smell like many of the other rooms. Was it possible that Gary had kept Winston there but moved him to a different location? If so, would he move him back? Maybe she could hide and watch. She would know when Winston came back, and she would know when Gary left. Maybe Gary had been watching her and the policeman and knew the coast was clear.

At first she thought it was ridiculous. But as she thought about it, she realized it was exactly something Gary would do. Why hadn't she acted when she first saw that church and felt it was an answer to prayer? She could already be with Winston! All the heartache and suffering could be over. And now, if she didn't act quickly, he might be gone again. She wasn't sure how long she had been wandering near the ravine while praying. She may have already wasted too much time. She had to go now. Right away! Should she find Jenna at least? Call the police? But she'd already been like the little boy who cried wolf, she thought.

She decided she would do the same thing she did when she went to the cave. She would text Jenna before she went inside, with instructions to call the police if she didn't hear back from her within fifteen minutes. That way, Jenna couldn't stop her from going, and the police would be quickly alerted in case of a problem. Her whereabouts would be known, and they would both be saved in a matter of minutes.

It seemed like a solid plan.

Chapter 38 ————————————————————————————

The Church

ALLIE WATCHED AND WAITED for a long time but didn't see anything. The church looked deserted. But she realized from her vantage point that Gary could be accessing the church from the opposite side. Although there were quite a lot of trees and bushes around the church, the foliage grew sparser away from it, not allowing a lot of options for her to hide or change positions. She fidgeted with nervousness, wanting to act but scared to death. Plus, she was afraid to break a window. Why hadn't she called the police?

While she watched and waited, she continually felt haunted by the image of that empty room. She saw it every time she closed her eyes. The room was large yet claustrophobic, possibly because it was so gloomy and cold, like a cavernous tomb. The feeling inside the church was eerie, unlike any church she had been in, but it had been abandoned. There was no pastor or worshipping congregation to fill it, take care of it, or care for the people who attended it. It was no longer a church. It was just a building—a building that had not been cared for in a long time.

She looked for all the possible ways to get in. The side door was solid glass. The front doors were solid wood. Most of the windows were large, with wooden cross-hatching. Even if she broke the glass, she would never fit through the diamond-shaped hole. She found a more conventional window. Gently, she tapped on it with a rock, and then harder and harder until it finally cracked. Then she used the rock to break through the cracked piece where she was able to unlock the window and slide it open. She texted

Jenna that she was entering the church, asking her to call the police if she didn't hear back in fifteen minutes. Then she slid through the window and into the eerie stillness of the church.

She had to be careful. What if Gary was here? The thought filled her with icy dread. She had hoped to never see Gary again. But her desire to see and help Winston outweighed her loathing of her husband. She pressed forward, looking for the stairway to the basement. She tiptoed, listening for voices or any sounds indicating another person was in the building. Nothing. Although, if only one person was in here, they would not be likely to make a sound, she thought.

Did she dare turn on a light? She felt like she was in the cave all over again. This time, the territory wasn't unfamiliar, but was somebody here? That was the unknown factor. She had to tread carefully just in case. She clicked on the light at the top of the staircase, illuminating the narrow passageway and wooden stairs leading to the basement. If Gary saw the light, he would come to investigate, and she would have a running start to get out of there and call 911.

Nothing. Not a sound. Slowly, carefully, she moved down the stairs, her hands trailing the sides of the walls barely a whisper. At the bottom, she craned her neck around the corner. Nothing. Just the few finished rooms at the far end, darkness, and a few more rooms roughed in with two-by-fours. Again, just a solitary naked light bulb to light the entire vast space.

Now briskly, urgently, she tiptoed to the heavy wooden door that led to the room she could see every time she closed her eyes. When she was here with the officer, the door had been open. Now it was closed. She shivered.

She peered at the door, looking for a lock. There! The door had a dead bolt mounted on the outside—just the thing to hold a prisoner. Had Gary installed that himself? Probably. She slid the lock open and looked inside. The room that had been empty except for a solitary chair now had a lumpy mass in the corner. Could it be?

"Winston?" she whispered. "Winston?" she asked with increasing certainty. The lumpy mass moved. Then a man sat up. Suddenly Allie felt intense fear. She looked around for a weapon, but the room was bare.

"Allie?"

She practically crumpled with relief, her legs like gelatin. The rush of adrenaline that had pumped through her left her feeling limp, but joy started to surge through her now, propelling her toward this man she loved.

"Winston!" She ran to him, throwing her arms around his neck. "Are you ok? Are you hurt? Let's get you out of here!"

Upstairs, a door slammed. Allie looked at Winston with wide eyes. "Quick!"

Winston scurried out of the sleeping bag, and Allie quickly arranged it to look like someone was still under it. They fled the room, locking the bolt behind them. They had just darted into a shadowy corner when Gary bounded down the stairs. Allie nearly gagged with the revulsion she felt for him, but she clamped a hand over her mouth. Gary unlocked the door and went in.

Allie had planned to lock him in the room, but then she realized Gary would have a key and that would immediately alert him to their presence. No, if they could just stay hidden until he left, they could make a safe and quiet getaway.

"No!" came an angry yell that left Allie cowering. Winston put a reassuring hand on her arm. She should have been the one comforting him after his horrible ordeal. He had been missing for four days already, and this was not a pleasant place to be. Allie quit quaking and held still as Gary rushed out of the room and bounded up the stairs two or three at a time. The door slammed again.

"Hurry! Let's get out of here!" Allie said urgently, grabbing Winston's arm. The tranquilizers had worn off an hour or two before, but Winston was dizzy and unsteady. They navigated the stairs slowly. Allie looked at her watch. Jenna may have already called the police, but Allie wasn't thinking straight and couldn't be sure.

"Come on, Winston," she encouraged as they left the building and headed down the street. "My car is just across the street and down the block a ways. Or would you like to wait here and I'll come pick you up?"

But Winston was already picking up the pace. "No, it's okay. It feels good to walk. I'm doing much better." Suddenly he stopped, body rigid. He pointed at Allie's car. "Allie! I saw movement. I think Gary is waiting in your car!"

They spun around and started running. "I wondered where he went!" Allie exclaimed, panicked. "Quick! This way. I know a place to hide," she said, thinking of the cave. She pulled out her cell phone and called the police. "Help! This is Allie Tackleman. I found Winston Grover, who was being held captive in West Haven Church on Rycart Avenue by Gary Tackleman.

And now he's chasing us. We are heading toward the river and ravine on foot. Please come quickly!"

Allie guided a stumbling Winston toward the river. He was weak, exhausted, and dehydrated, even though the tranquilizer had worn off. They were fortunate they'd had more than a half-a-block head start and Gary didn't know where they were going. The rolling hills kept them mostly hidden, but Gary was keeping to the top of the hills, allowing him to spot them. The temperatures in this desert town had soared, further zapping Winston's strength. Finally, they reached the river near the cave. Oh, where were the police? Allie wondered. Gary was closing in, and if they went into the cave, they would be trapped. Winston was too tired to fight. Allie felt cornered and defeated, not knowing how long the police would take or what Gary would do if he caught them. They were running out of real estate as they approached the river and were getting boxed in at the ravine.

෴ ෴

Winston peered over the ledge to the river. Thinking it looked deep enough, he was just about to make the leap. "How about a shortcut?" he asked.

"No!" Allie yelled.

He looked up just in time and backed away from the ledge. Allie pointed to the river. He could see a few rocks through the murkiness. It was not nearly as deep as it appeared, he noted with alarm. From this height, he could have suffered significant injury.

He watched as Allie traversed the rugged cliffside upstream and around the bend to a different spot, looking back to make sure Winston had followed. She pointed. The river roared with white-capped rapids at this point, and Winston looked at her questioningly. This spot looked even more dangerous than the last. She nodded and reached for his hand. They counted to three and leapt, landing with a large splash, the sound drowned out by the rush of the water. They surfaced and were carried downstream in the direction they had just come from.

"Should we keep riding this current away to safety?" Winston shouted.

"I think we should try, but I'm scared he will gain on us. You're so weak and tired," Allie answered. "He wasn't far behind us."

Expecting to see Gary's unwelcome face at any moment, they were reaching the spot where Winston had almost jumped.

"Quick! Let's get against the cliff where he can't see us! He probably wouldn't expect us to jump but maybe run a different direction," Allie said urgently.

But Winston had a different idea.

"Let's stay here. Find the deepest place you can and have only your head visible above the water. Perhaps Gary will be fooled as easily as I was," he said. "If he's hurt, he can't hurt us."

"No, let's hide. What if he shoots at us?" Allie asked.

"I don't think he has a gun. So far he's used brute force, drugs, and withholding food from me. And I know he wants you back. I don't think he would take the chance of shooting at you," Winston said.

Suddenly, Gary's face appeared, purple with rage. He spotted them and laughed, greasy head thrown back. Winston shuddered in revulsion.

"Darling, I've found you at last!" Gary shouted. "I can't wait to take you home and get back to our normal life together. Maybe we can still get to the fertility clinic so we can start our family."

He thought that appealing? Winston was disgusted. Poor Allie! Winston looked over at her, but she was turned away. Winston wasn't sure if she couldn't stand the sight of Gary or if she was scared what would happen if Gary jumped in after them.

But Winston wanted his plan to work. "You'll get her back over my dead body," Winston yelled.

Gary roared in anger. "That can be arranged!" And he made a running jump into the river.

Allie screamed.

Winston held his breath, suddenly horrified by what was about to happen.

Chapter 39

Revelations

GARY'S ARMS WINDMILLED AS he jumped toward Winston, who half-swam, half-scrambled backward through the slippery rocks. Gary's eyes widened as he suddenly saw the rocks and the shallowness of the river.

Allie covered her eyes and turned away. Gary's scream echoed off the cliffs for what seemed like an eternity. But that sound was far more welcome than the crunching blow of Gary's body smacking against solid rock—a boulder barely hidden under the surface of the water. Upon impact, a new scream rose up from the canyon, and then Gary crumpled. Allie finally turned around, but she was unprepared to see her husband lying in a twisted heap. His eyes were wide, and he was pleading for help.

"Go, Allie! Run and get help," Winston called. "I will stay with him, help him if I can." Winston had already reached Gary's side and was determining if there was any possible way to safely move the suffering man into a less excruciating position.

Allie's wet sneakers fought for purchase as she slid and scrambled up the rocky slope around the bend. She ran as fast as she could, tripping occasionally, falling only once as she searched for the policemen who should surely be here by now.

At the top of the ravine, red-and-blue lights flashed, and a couple of officers were running toward the river when she found them and explained what had happened to Gary. They determined that sending a helicopter was the best option. Once again, she made the mad dash back to the scene.

She scrambled down the slope and into the river, sloshing over to where Winston was attempting to comfort her suffering husband. Gary was in agonizing pain, but his eyes lit up when he saw Allie, and she tenderly took his hand. She whispered encouraging words and explained that help was on its way. As the policemen watched the scene from the top of the ridge, the helicopter appeared above them. The officers guided the helicopter to land nearby, and Allie was astonished at how quickly they were able to load Gary into the helicopter.

"Do you think he will be okay?" she yelled to Winston over the wind created by the rotors.

"He's still alive," Winston answered. "But he is in a lot of pain. I tried to comfort him while you were gone, but I didn't dare move him. His back looked crooked and possibly broken, and I didn't want to risk further damage to his spine."

"It's too awful!" Allie exclaimed, bursting into tears.

"Ma'am! Do you want to ride with him?" The paramedic yelled over the din.

Allie wiped her eyes, nodded, and scrambled toward the helicopter. She pointed back to Winston. "That man needs hospital care also. He has been held captive for several days and could be severely dehydrated. He's also been badly beaten and concussed."

The paramedic ran over to Winston, quickly assessing his poor condition—although it was nothing compared to his already loaded-up counterpart.

"Jack! Bring another gurney! We've got another one to transport!"

"Don't be ridiculous. I'm all right," Winston muttered, but the paramedic was already in motion, directing him to the helicopter.

Allie hopped aboard, concerned for both men. She held Gary's hand. "Gary, I'm here. We're going to get you patched up good as new," she promised. Gary didn't grasp her hand, nor did he turn his head, but he followed her every move with his eyes. He grunted a reply. When he closed his eyes, Allie quickly checked him and looked at the equipment he was hooked up to. When he drifted off to sleep or lost consciousness because of the pain— Allie wasn't sure which—she asked the paramedic if he thought Gary would be all right.

"I can't make any promises, but I think so," he said. "His vitals are strong, but I suspect half of the bones in his body are broken. I'm Steve, by the way."

Allie gasped and put a hand to her mouth. "Half? How awful. How long will he be in pain?"

"It's going to be a long, painful road to recovery," Steve admitted. "What happened anyway? Did he fall off that cliff or did he jump? Did he not know how shallow it was right there?" Suddenly light sparked in his green eyes, and he held up a hand. "I think I know," he said. He turned to Allie, then motioned to Winston. "You said that he had been held captive, so I can only assume he got away with your help and that this guy chased you down into the canyon. You had safely gotten into the river, but he tried to take a shortcut and—"

Allie and Winston both nodded.

"So why was he holding you captive? Or would you rather save your story for the police?" All of a sudden, Steve's eyes lit up again, the green eyes looking greener. "Oh, of course." He looked at Allie and Winston carefully. "You're the lawyer who has been missing the last couple of days. And you," he pointed at Allie, "you're the mysterious woman who disappeared at the beach a couple months ago. And that is your husband, who was frantically searching for you." But suddenly the clear eyes filled with confusion. Try as he might, he could not place the remaining pieces of the puzzle. Where had she gone when she left the beach? And why was her husband holding another man captive? It didn't make sense.

"You are right again," Allie confirmed, though she didn't elaborate. She couldn't believe a lost, unknown woman from South Dakota would have so many people aware of her circumstances, but perhaps with so many aware of her situation, she could somehow use it as a way to help others. She was satisfied when Winston was thoroughly checked out midflight and given an IV.

"I'm starving," he whispered to Allie.

"That's a good sign," Steve volunteered. "We'll get you some food as soon as we arrive. When was the last time you ate?"

"What day is it?" Winston asked.

"Friday."

"I guess Wednesday, then."

Allie gasped. "He didn't feed you? What did he do to you?"

Winston shrugged, downplaying the horror. "I got to eat once. He withheld food to get me to tell him where you were."

Allie knew Gary's games. "So if you told him, he would let you eat, but if you didn't, you had to sit there and watch him eat," she said quietly.

"Pretty much. So yeah . . . I could use some food!"

Allie gave him a hug. "That was so heroic of you. I'm so sorry you had to endure that." She didn't even realize she was crying.

"Me? I was only with the guy for four days. You were the one who spent, what, like, five or seven years with the creep? I'm sorry you had to endure that." He reached out and hugged her back.

"So he was abusive and you ran away from him at the beach?" the paramedic asked.

Allie nodded.

"How did he find you? I thought the police declared you legally dead."

"I was unfortunate enough to have my picture taken at a high-profile event. Gary saw it on the news," Allie told Steve.

"And presuming he was also in the photograph," Steve motioned to Winston, "he tracked him down to find you."

Suddenly, Gary screamed. Steve bolted to his bedside, checking him and the equipment, then added some morphine into his IV drip. Gary settled back down.

When they landed, Gary was whisked away. Allie was torn. Should she follow Gary or Winston?

"Go!" Winston waved, making the decision for her.

Allie scrambled out of the helicopter and followed the disappearing gurney through the automatic glass doors at the ER.

"Family only from this point," the nurse said, barring her way.

"I'm his wife," she answered and was immediately granted access.

The doctor wasted no time feeling his bones and arranging for X-rays. Fortunately, Gary was awake. "Can you feel that?" he asked, poking his foot. Gary shook his head.

Allie stepped out while the X-rays were taken but came back in and grasped Gary's hand again when they were complete.

He looked up at her. "I'm so glad I got to see you again, to be with you again. I missed you so much. I love you," he said.

Allie was surprised. She couldn't remember the last time Gary told her he loved her. She was touched in a way that surprised her. He had some good in him, but it had been stripped away for a long time, buried under his own wall of pain, abuse, and hardships. And while she had turned to God for help and to help her with her heartaches, he had turned away and cursed God, instead relying on his own strength. The contrast in the results of those decisions was startling.

He was looking at her with pleading eyes, but she couldn't give him the answer he wanted. She couldn't lie, but she could comfort him. "Gary," she took a long, steadying breath and mustered up her courage. "I forgive you."

᭢ ᭢

His eyes widened and then filled with heavy, wet tears. His body convulsed painfully as he let the tears seep out. He thought about the way he had mistreated his wife. He recalled the victory he'd felt when Alexandria's mom had believed him and doubted her own daughter. He thought of how he had cursed and tried to use his adoptive parents. He thought about the times he had hit, kicked, smacked, grabbed, and manhandled this petite woman in front of him. She had done nothing but worked long and hard and put up with his abuse. And now she was *forgiving* him?

Forgiving him for what? For encouraging his own wife to do her duties? For using force to encourage her obedience? He felt indignant. But amidst his current suffering, he couldn't lie to himself. He had inflicted physical and emotional pain on his wife—had done so every single day—and now he was paying for that huge mistake. This time his crocodile tears were for himself, for all the pain he was in and had yet to endure on the long road of recovery. But at least he had Alexandria back, he thought. She would see him through, nurse him back to health. He wouldn't be able to run the ranch for quite a while, and Alexandria would come back and do that, he thought with satisfaction. Finally, he could take it easy and enjoy watching her do all the work again.

The morphine kicked in, and he drifted off to sleep, smiling at his future with her.

Chapter 40 ───────────────────────────

Consequences

WHEN HE AWOKE AGAIN, Alexandria was gone. He kept asking for her. He kept trying to move but couldn't because of so many broken bones and casts. Was she already back home, taking care of the ranch? No one would answer his questions, instead telling him to just settle down and relax.

He couldn't wait to see her again, to know she would be by his side to help him through it.

"Doc?" Gary asked. He wasn't sure how many days had gone by. "How come I can't feel my legs? You said the bones are mending. I don't understand."

The doctor grimly pulled a stool close to Gary's bed. "There is something I haven't told you. I didn't want it to interfere with your recovery." Gary wondered if he had cancer or some disease they'd discovered through the blood work. He watched the doctor screw up the courage to deliver the next blow. "Gary, you are paralyzed from the waist down. When you jumped into the river, you snapped some of the key vertebrae in your back, and you won't have any feeling or movement in your legs again."

Gary gaped. "I'm paralyzed? He lifted his arms and dropped them again, looking at the movement he had left.

The doctor nodded. "You are fortunate to have complete movement in your upper body. One more vertebra and you would have been a quadriplegic."

Gary shivered. This was awful. Devastating. But it could have been much worse. "Does my wife know?" he asked.

The doctor nodded once more. "Are you ready to talk to her, or do you need time to process this news?"

"I'm ready now," he said. He didn't think he could wait one more minute to see his wife. She was all he ever thought about in his waking moments. Things were going to be different from now on, he decided. He wasn't going to be harsh or demanding. He was going to be grateful that she would be able to do the things he couldn't do for himself. He was going to have to take care of himself and his needs and be as independent as possible because Alexandria was going to have to run the ranch singlehandedly, and that was a huge undertaking.

She walked in an hour later, looking absolutely stunning. Her hair had grown longer and was bleached blonde by the California sun. It cascaded across her shoulders in golden waves. Her eyes looked sparkling and intelligent—nothing like the dull, discouraged eyes he was used to seeing. Her clothes were stylish and expensive and flattered her filled-out figure. She was no longer just skin and bones. Now she studied him with a look of compassion. She came and took his hand.

"You look lovely, but where have you been? Haven't you been running the ranch?" he asked. "I've missed you."

"I was busy with my college classes, wrapping up a variety of assignments, and working for Winston."

Gary started. Winston—the guy he'd kidnapped in order to get his wife back. Winston, the *lawyer*. Was he going to come after him? Would there be legal repercussions? Jail time? Gary shuddered. What would they do to a paralyzed man in prison? Would he even have to go? He did not want to know.

Gary was contrite. He had completely glossed over the consequences of his actions in his quest to fill his dreams of a future with Alexandria. And now he was paralyzed. Now he had no idea what the future held. But he could ask his wife.

"Alexandria? Did you know I was paralyzed? What's going to happen to me? To us?" he asked.

She nodded, taking his hand once more. "Gary, I'm so grateful you're ok, that it wasn't worse. But I don't want to be married to you anymore. I never wanted to marry you in the first place. I felt like I was forced into it."

Gary hung his head. A few tears trickled down his cheeks. She squeezed his hand and continued. "I have not been unfaithful to you, but I do love someone else. Very much. I have built a life here. I have gone to college. I have made friends. I have helped Winston with the cases he is working on. I have been studying social work so that I can help others in situations similar to what I was in." She stopped and studied Gary, looking for any indication that he knew what he had done to her was wrong. She saw sadness and remorse.

"You already forgave me," Gary said. "But I want you to know I have thought about what you said over and over. I felt it was my right to treat you like I did because you were my wife, but I realize that those days are long gone—and they were never right in the first place. I am sorry. I truly am. And I will treat you with love and respect and kindness in the future, and I hope you can grow to love me."

Allie patted his hand. "I realize that I do love you. And I think I understand you. And I do forgive you," she said, rubbing his arm. "But I won't ever be able to forget what you did. And because I won't ever be able to forget the past, it will always be a roadblock, preventing us from having a real marriage. I want a real marriage, Gary. If you truly love me and you've truly changed, will you please let me have a divorce?"

Gary looked shocked.

"I'm going to let you think that over," Allie said, getting up.

"No! I don't need any time to think it over," he said, his voice gathering strength. "You are my wife—through sickness and health, joy and sorrow. We've had some sorrow, and now I'm in poor health. I need you to take care of me. I can't let you divorce me. I need you to run the ranch."

Allie was sad. For all his thoughts of change and forgiveness, he was still selfish. "Is that why you want to stay married to me? So that I can take care of you and run the ranch?"

"Yes. I mean, no. I need you, but I also love you."

"When have you ever shown me you love me?" Allie asked, curiously.

Gary just stared, then said, "Well, for Christmas, I got you that new saddle."

"So that I could take care of the ranch," she said with a sigh. "That is not love, Gary. But I will tell you what I will do for you. I will see that Sam remains your ranch foreman. I will see that you have a nurse and a cook. And I will also pay your medical expenses," she said gently. "And I will have Pastor Willis check on you regularly and teach you about Jesus Christ, who suffered far beyond what you are suffering. He was my one true and only Friend until I moved here. And he will be your Friend as well."

Gary's eyes had hardened. Had his heart as well? Allie wondered. "And if I say no to a divorce?" he sneered.

Allie was taken aback that he would revert to his old self so quickly. Did she bring out the worst in him? Or maybe he didn't know how to accept kindness.

"I will do all those things whether we are married or not," she said.

"And will you live with your boyfriend whether we are married or not?" he asked.

"I will remain in California whether we are married or not," she said. She had tried to control her mounting anger. She didn't want to say something she'd regret, but that last comment was too hurtful. She wanted to be with Winston, but as his wife, and this horrid man stood in her way. "I never want to see you or the ranch again," she couldn't stop herself from saying. "And if you don't divorce me, you won't be spending any time at the ranch either. I will file charges for all of the abuse you have inflicted on me over the years, to add to the charges Winston will also be filing for kidnapping, assault, the attempted murder of his butler, and breaking and entering. Either way, I don't think I will ever have to see your horrid face again."

She left.

And she never went to the hospital to visit him again.

But the divorce papers were signed and delivered to the office of Grover & Grover.

Chapter 41 ————————————————————————

Answered Prayers

WINSTON HAD TO KNOW the rest of the story.

"What happened?" he asked. "How did you find me? Gary said no one on earth would figure out where I was. He claimed he'd totally outsmarted everyone."

"True. But I didn't figure out where you were. Like he said, no one on earth could. But God in heaven knew where you were. I prayed with all my might, and then I just knew with every fiber of my being. A picture came, like a snapshot, and I knew where you were."

She told Winston about finding the cave and then explained how she felt Winston was in that church and how she'd had to wait to get in. She explained how Gary had seen her and moved Winston—Winston didn't remember that, so he didn't know where he was moved to—and then returned to the church. She kept seeing that room over and over and felt driven to go there.

"An absolute miracle," Winston exclaimed.

"Yes! So do you believe in answered prayers?"

"Allie, from the moment I met you, you were so filled with faith. I couldn't deny that God had answered your prayers. I still can't explain the urge I felt that day at the beach to rescue you. It must have been God answering your prayer. And then this particular prayer saved my life." He paused, looking into her luminous eyes. "I hope God will answer the prayer that's in my heart right now."

"Of course He will," she said, wondering what he meant and looking at him with questioning eyes.

"The biggest thing I can think to ask for is that you, Allie, consent to by my wife."

Her mouth formed a perfect O, then broke out into an enormous smile.

"I think I can help God answer that particular prayer," she said and kissed him.

Two Years Later

ALLIE SMILED AS SHE reread the Christmas card and set it on the mantel.

"Good morning, sweetheart," Winston said, smiling and breezing into the room. "Who's the card from?"

"From Gary," she answered, eyes twinkling. "Want me to read it to you?"

"Of course." While Allie's back was turned, he tucked a few untidily wrapped gifts under the tree, checking to make sure she was still distracted.

Allie held the card up and read, "Dear Winston and Allie—"

"Even he is calling you Allie now," Winston noticed.

Allie's smile grew wider.

Dear Winston and Allie,

Merry Christmas to two of my most favorite people in the world. I am doing well, and I am still enjoying last year's gift very much. I just had to share the good news. Through the oil painting classes you gave me for Christmas, I have found joy and purpose in life. Through connections with a woman in my congregation, I am going to have my first showing at a gallery. Isn't that exciting? And I have you two to thank for it, as I do for all the many good things in my life—my home, my nurse; my cook, who I hope to soon make my wife; and my happiness in finding and accepting the Lord as my Savior. I don't deserve to be this happy after all the awful things I have done. Thank you again for your forgiveness and for putting me on the right path. I wish you the merriest of Christmases.

Love, Gary

Allie held up the small painting he had created for them—a beautiful landscape of the South Dakota ranch with cattle dotted across the prairie under a wide blue sky full of puffy clouds.

"That's beautiful," Winston complimented. His gifts to her now safely hidden under the tree, Winston drew close, wrapping his arms around her and admiring the painting. "I think he will like this year's Christmas gift also," he said.

"Me too," Allie agreed. She had talked to Gary's fiancée, and they were throwing them their dream wedding this spring.

A loud cry rent the air, and they both rushed out of the room, playfully jockeying for position to be the first to the nursery to scoop their son out of his crib.

Allie let Winston win. The sight of him with his son was too precious not to witness. Besides, she got to spend more time with Winston Jaymeson Grover Jr. than Winston did since she stayed home with him, only joining Winston at the office for certain cases she assisted with. And fortunately, Winston always worked reasonable hours. He couldn't wait to get home in the evenings.

"Merry Christmas, Junior," Winston exclaimed, picking up the little one and holding him close.

"Da-da," said the nine-month-old with a sloppy grin that showed four teeth.

Winston beamed at him proudly. He placed his son over his head and held on to his feet to give him a bouncy piggyback ride. Junior immediately started to squeal. Winston laughed, then looked at Allie. "Well, honey, now that we're all awake, should we go open some gifts?"

Allie nodded, although she couldn't think of a single thing that could be stashed under the Christmas tree that would make her any happier than she felt at this moment. And she told her husband so.

He quirked an eyebrow. "Surely there's something. In fact, the question I should be asking is what have you prayed for this time?" he asked affectionately.

Allie couldn't hide her smile. She *had* prayed for something. And he was about to find out the surprise.

Winston waited expectantly. Whatever it was, he would do his best to help answer her prayer.

"First, unwrap this gift, and then I will tell you what I prayed for," she said, handing him a small rectangular box.

Winston tore off the wrapping paper and pulled out a small object. Realization dawned as he stared at it, and his eyes practically popped out of his head. But sure enough, the test he held in his hands indicated a positive result.

"You're pregnant?" he asked, his heart hoping for her confirmation. "Is that what you prayed for?"

"Yes, but I was a little more specific than that. I prayed for a daughter," she said, her eyes shining with love, hope, and happiness.

"I guess we'll paint the nursery pink in about six months, then! Because if you prayed for it, I have little doubt that your prayer will be answered," Winston said, laughing. They embraced with Junior snuggled in the middle.